MOUSE HEART

FLEUR HITCHCOCK

For Isla, for lending me your mum

First published in the UK in 2022 by Nosy Crow Ltd
The Crow's Nest, 14 Baden Place
Crosby Row, London, SE1 1YW, UK

Nosy Crow Eireann Ltd
44 Orchard Grove, Kenmare
Co Kerry, V93 FY22, Ireland

Nosy Crow and associated logos are trademarks and/or registered
trademarks of Nosy Crow Ltd.

Text copyright © Fleur Hitchcock, 2022
Cover artwork © Ben Mantle, 2022

The right of Fleur Hitchcock to be identified as the author of this
work has been asserted.

ISBN: 978 1 78800 948 5

A CIP catalogue record for this book is available from the British Library.

Printed and bound in Great Britain by Clays Ltd, Elcograf S.p.A.
Typeset by Tiger Media

Papers used by Nosy Crow are made from
wood grown in sustainable forests.

MIX
Paper from
responsible sources
FSC® C018072

1 3 5 7 9 10 8 6 4 2

www.nosycrow.com

The mouse may sometimes help the lion in need.

Proverb

'Tis a bold mouse that nestles in the cat's ear.

Proverb

These events take place during the reign of Queen Anne II

Prologue

A harbour.

All around, tall-sailed ships creak.

Night creatures scuttle away.

The cobbles glow pink. Not from the crime about to happen, but with the coming of the September dawn.

From what is left of the shadows, two figures emerge.

A blade is raised and a scream splits the empty quayside, scaring sleeping gulls into the air.

A moment later — uproar.

Feet clatter through the alleyways.

Run. Run!

Chapter 1

I've waited half an hour for Valentina. Watched a shaft of morning sunlight sundial on and off the stage while the seagulls battled overhead.

"Maybe she's forgotten us, Dog," I say, rubbing the grey ears of my old friend. He opens an eye and lets his head fall heavier on my leg. Outside, a church bell chimes seven times and someone uses the pump at the back of the theatre. Pumping, washing. Pumping, washing.

I shrug Dog off my knee and unsheathe my little rapier. I stand by the line of sunlight and let the blade dance in the air, swooping and sliding, catching the sunbeams and flicking the fractured light across the balconies that ring the stage. I parry, I lunge, driving the point towards my unseen foe and twisting the blade home.

"*Touché! Brava! Bene, bene!*" a scrawny figure calls from the shadows. It's Mr Hawkin, the man who runs the theatre company. "What skill, what promise!" He clamps a broom handle to his chest, claps, and a crow takes off from the side of the stage and flies out through the open roof.

I'm staring up at it when my blade is whisked from my hand by a second sword. I race to grab it but it spins and falls, to land embedded in the wooden boards next to Mr Hawkin's shoe.

"I say!" he says, jumping aside. Dog barks once and leaps from the stage to the sawdust floor below.

"There, poppet!" says Valentina, advancing across the stage. "Get out of that one!"

"How did you do that?" I look up at her.

"Skill, Mouse. Natural skill." She plucks a black hat from her head and bows. As she rises, her hair bubbles free in a copper cloud, bright against her black clothing. "So sorry I'm late. Now – ready?"

She lowers the point of her sword so that it rests on the third button on my shirt.

"Come on, sweetie," she whispers. "Don't let your

heart rule your head."

She pushes damp cuffs up her arms and the pale hairs catch the light. I watch her elbow – I know that it will flicker before she moves.

I step back, she advances, and I drop to the ground hands first and flip myself under her sword to the other side of the stage.

"*Brava! Brava!*" Mr Hawkin claps as I grasp the hilt of my sword and yank it from the wood.

"*Allez!*" shouts Valentina. "Go, Mouse, go!"

We circle each other. Valentina glides over the boards. We clash.

"Oh, splendid!" Mr Hawkin stamps his broom on the stage.

I hear angry crows above and running feet outside but my gaze is fixed on her sword.

She feints left; I leap to the right.

"Help! Help!" Sudden shouts come from outside the theatre. Caught mid-stroke, we freeze.

"What—" Valentina drops her sword.

The side door of the theatre crashes open and Walter staggers in, his usually sunny face rigid with fear. "I didn't do it!" he cries, stepping into the circle of sunlight, holding up his fingers and examining them as if he doesn't understand where the blood could have come from. "Help me! Mouse, Valentina.

Help me!"

"*Giove!*" exclaims Mr Hawkin. "Is that ... real blood?"

Walter falls to his knees and holds out his palms. They're thick with it. "Hide me!" he says. "They think I did it."

Chapter 2

While Valentina charges into action, rubbing Walter's footprints from the sawdust, I'm paralysed.

Mr Hawkin shuts and bars the side door and almost as soon as he does, someone pounds on the main doors, sharp and angry.

"Mouse?" Walter looks up at me. He's crying.

"Let's wash it off," I say, burying my fear and dragging him to his feet.

"No time for that," says Valentina. "We have to hide him. The costume store."

Running with his hands out as if they belong to someone else, Walter races up the stairs and we follow him.

"Where?" he says, stopping in the doorway of the costume store.

Valentina points to the largest of the hampers.

From down below I can hear men shouting and Mr Hawkin bellows, "Hold on, hold on, I'm coming, but we're closed, you know!"

Valentina and I throw everything out of the hamper while Walter stands staring at the blood clotting on his fingernails.

"I don't even know who she is."

"Who?" says Valentina, grunting as she pulls out the heavy velvet cloaks folded in the bottom of the hamper.

"The woman – I think she was already dead. It was … it was horrible."

The shouting intensifies. "They're in the theatre," I say, dragging the empty hamper to the back of the room. "Who are those men?"

"I don't know. The law?" whimpers Walter. "I'm scared, Mouse."

I grip his bloody hand and hold it tight. I should say something comforting, but instead I'm panicking.

Valentina leans forward and kisses the top of his head. "You'll be fine. Just get in there."

Wiping his hands on his jacket, Walter clambers

over the side of the hamper. There are smears of blood on the wicker. I heap the cloaks on his head and Valentina wipes the blood away with a handkerchief. We jam the lid on the hamper, throw curtains over the top and rush to sit quietly at the sewing table under a little window.

Valentina pulls a frilled dress over from the side, heaping it across her legs, and threads a needle. She starts sewing a strip of lace to the cuffs.

"Slow your breathing," she whispers. "And don't panic. They'll be looking for panic."

I glance up at her.

She points back at the fabric. She seems to know what we need to do, as if she's tangled with people like this before.

Filling my hands with cloth and pins I randomly pin the bottom of a dress. I must keep my fingers moving. Otherwise they'll shake.

Dog sits beside me, ears twitching, but his tail lies flat on the floor. He looks up at me as if I can explain the sounds coming from below.

Feet thump on the staircases and I hear Mr Hawkin protest. Glancing up at the door, I spot a red handprint. Oh no! But then I remember it must come from the murder play we did last. Walter's hands were dripping that time too. And Valentina did a whole chunk where she tried to wash blood off her palms.

It was really good.

I got murdered.

I quite often get murdered.

The audiences like plays with murders in them.

Breathe, Mouse, breathe.

I'm trying hard not to think about the men.

Don't let the fear in.

Bang!

The door to the costume store swings open and two men in heavy grey coats burst in.

"Perfect!" says the one in front. He's short, almost bald and grizzled. He narrows his eyes as he surveys the lines of hanging costumes. "Lots of itty-bitty hiding places for our villain."

"Our … murderer," says his partner, rolling the "R" in the middle of the word. This man's tall and young-looking, with a sprouty beard and raggedy teeth to match.

"Quite correct," says the first. "We are indeed seeking a mur-de-rer."

"He could easily be in here…" The second man pulls a sword and gestures to a pile of sacking. The sword is not like the little one I fight with, but a long, heavy, mean kind of sword that would run a person through. "Or in here!" He pokes the blade into the holes at the top of the smallest hamper.

"I could even do a little of this!" He lunges and the sword runs smoothly through the layers of costumes inside.

"No!" squawks Mr Hawkin. "Those are our livelihood! You can't do that!"

"Show us where he is and we won't." The young man pauses, his sword in mid-air. His gaze is flicking all around the room.

"We know he's in the theatre – we saw him come in," says the older one from the door.

"There's a back entrance, you know," I say as loudly as I dare.

The grey one looks around the eaves. "Did someone speak?" he says. He comes over to me and examines the cloth in my hands. He reaches for it and I let him pick it up. "What's this?"

"A costume," I mumble.

"A costume." He nods his head. He smells stale and there's a fresh trickle of sweat running down from his ear to the grubby top of his shirt collar. "So why is there a row of pins right through the middle? Eh? Not a hem, not attaching two things to each other – just right through the middle."

"Stop it!" says Valentina. "She's just a child – while I sew, she amuses herself with the pins. Is that a problem?" she says the final word as if she thinks the man is stupid.

He leans forward, his nose meeting hers.

"Rot!" he says. "I know you theatre types. You can climb on the roof by the time you're weaned. You're on stage before you can talk. So don't lie to me, pretty lady, or I'll have you."

Valentina brushes his face to the side. It's not a slap, but it's firm, and then she stands. She's far taller than him and I can see it doesn't please him one bit.

Beyond them, the other one has opened the costume hampers. All of them. He's jabbing each one in turn. The sword dips in and out, slicing through the fabric below.

"Anyone in there?" he says, as if he's playing hide and seek with a small child. "Come out to play, little one — we just want to clap you in irons!"

I stare at the large hamper. I can't help it. And I know I'm probably showing all the signs of panic. I unclench my fist and sneak a glance at my palms. They're smeared with blood from Walter's hand.

The room is holding its breath. Mr Hawkin is wide-eyed, staring at the mess of costumes. I'm guessing he's more worried about the costumes than Walter.

Valentina is fuming. I can feel it.

The man with the sword reaches the large hamper.

"Wakey-wakey, little man. Time to get out of the basket!"

"Stop!" Red fingers emerge, grip the side of the hamper and Walter, snow-faced, stands. He's shaking.

"Out you get," says the man. "Here." He holds out his hand as if Walter is an elderly woman needing help down from a horse. "Now, that was silly, wasn't it? We could just have arrested you without making holes in all these pretty clothes."

Chapter 3

I watch as they trap Walter's wrists in heavy metal rings.

I stand by as they drag Walter down the stairs and then push him from the stage to the pit. He lands badly and limps for a few paces, but the two men don't care.

Nobody's doing anything to stop it. Valentina and Mr Hawkin are just watching.

Without warning the words explode out of me. "You can't!" I shout. "You can't take Walter."

"Oh yes we can," says the short one, pushing me back. "Oh yes we can. I'm Jameson and he's Stuart.

We work for the queen and you're a nothing."

A nothing?

I dart under the man's arms and leap down into the pit, grabbing Walter's coat-tails and hanging on as tight as I can. Then I hook my elbow round Walter's, and Dog jumps down beside me and takes Walter's sleeve in his teeth, pulling him towards the stage. *We can do this, we can get him back.* Walter bends his knees. We slump together on the sawdust of the theatre floor. Dead weights, entangled.

"You're being quite a nuisance," says Stuart, the tall one. He jumps down next to me and picks me up under my armpits, yanking me away from Walter. As he swings me round I grab his arm and try to sink my teeth into it but he pulls my head back using my hair as a handle. Finally he draws his sword and points it at me. "Now, stay there, you!"

Dog leaps, but Jameson is there now and kicks him aside, and Dog skids through the sawdust, struggling to stay upright. He suddenly looks really old.

I sit with my back to the stage, licking blood from my lip, keeping my face as hard as the earth. Jameson shoves open the main doors and Stuart marches Walter outside, his sword-point in the small of Walter's back.

"Bye-bye, all!" says Jameson. "Oh yes, before you start calling in your powerful friends, remember –

harbouring a criminal is an offence. We could overlook our little search – or we could not. It depends…"
Doffing his three-cornered hat, he gives us a mocking bow and waves a cheery goodbye. He slams the door shut behind him.

There's an awful silence in the theatre. Mr Hawkin stares at the door as if Walter might come back through to deliver his punchline.

But he doesn't.

Chapter 4

The silence lasts a second longer before Mr Hawkin erupts.

"What in heaven's name just happened?" he demands.

"I don't know," says Valentina. She looks shocked, but not as shocked as Mr Hawkin, who has turned chalk white.

"What did that boy get involved in? This is not good, not good at all. Think of the reputation of the theatre – a murderer in our midst? How – how..." Mr Hawkin can't think of the word.

"Walter wouldn't kill anyone!" I shout, fighting

down a surge of furious tears.

"That blood on his hands came from somewhere," says Valentina.

A figure slips through the door from the back of the theatre and stops in the deep shade of the stage curtain. It's Kwadwo, the man who fixes everything and everyone in the building. He peers around the side of the curtain, checking, I know, to see if the soldiers have gone. If he's hiding, he's not doing a very good job; his dark-brown face is shiny and his cheeks and forehead reflect the light, as does his nose. And Kwadwo has a very long nose. Longer even than Mr Hawkin's. Dog raises his head, moans and lets his head fall again. He likes Kwadwo. I like Kwadwo. He's kind. He's my friend.

"What just happened?" He steps out into the sun, impeccably dressed; neat, buff breeches and clean stockings beneath a kingfisher-blue jacket. Unlike anyone else in the theatre Kwadwo is always presentable. "I heard shouting."

"The law has taken Walter," says Mr Hawkin.

"They think he murdered someone," I mutter.

"Walter?" says Kwadwo, running his fingers through his close-cropped hair. "Walter's the gentlest man I ever met. I don't believe this. Who would he even want to murder?"

He's right. Walter's not the murdering kind. He's the kindest, sweetest man. He looks after fledgling chicks and rescues drowned kittens. I was one of them. When I was a few hours old, Dog found me mewling inside a costume hamper, and it was Walter who washed the velvet dress I was wrapped in and tried to feed me. He was the one who named me Mouse after the field mice that shared my velvet dress, and persuaded the rest of the theatre company that they could bring up a baby. He was only twelve.

"We don't know much," says Mr Hawkin, leaning towards Kwadwo and lowering his voice. "It seems..."

I watch Mr Hawkin embellish the tale. He acts something out with a broom, thrusting at the air.

Valentina sighs. "It's all very unexpected. I feel quite..." she says, and runs off across the theatre towards the stairs.

For a moment I'm on my own. I wipe my eyes on my sleeve and try to keep fear at arm's length.

A sharp little voice scratches across the sawdust. "Crybaby!"

It's Eve. One of the Hawkin children. She and her brother Adam are usually together. Her in front, him behind. Eve is ... poisonous. Adam's her kinder shadow.

I pull my collar up and bury my head between my

knees. Dog settles alongside me and blows hot breath in my ear.

"Dog. Here, Dog," she calls.

Dog ignores her.

"Why don't you play with me?" says Eve in a plaintive voice. I peer around my collar. She's sitting on the side of the stage with her hands in her lap, her feet crossed at the ankle. Innocence.

"Go away!" I snap.

"Mama!" Eve patters away into the shadows at the back of the gallery where the Hawkin family live. I hear the door slam and Eve's wounded voice pleading with her mother about Dog.

Adam, far more ragged than his sister, emerges from their quarters to stare at me.

"Mouse?" he says. "I saw Walter. I'm..." He doesn't seem to know what he is. His face says he's sorry. He tries a wonky smile but wipes his face clean when I don't smile back.

"Mouse!" Valentina arrives alongside me in a cloud of perfume and powder. She's changed her clothes; she's wearing a russet dress that almost matches the red of her hair. She reaches around my shoulders and hugs me properly, closely, pressing my head to her chest. I'm slightly aware that Adam is still watching.

"Walter," is all I can say.

"It'll be all right, little rabbit."

"Will it?" I swallow. I want to believe her. It's so easy to believe Valentina. She knows so much about the world. "And what about harbouring a criminal like the man said? Will they put us in prison too?"

"I don't know," she says, pursing her lips. "I don't think they can imprison us all, can they, sweetie? Think how big the prison would have to be to contain Mr H. Just huge!" She smiles and gently prods the end of my hot nose.

"What do you think happened?" I ask.

Valentina stares into the air over my head. "I expect Walter came upon someone in trouble. Being Walter, he tried to help. Poor man — he should have walked on."

"But what'll happen to him?"

She goes still, staring up at the circle of sky above the theatre. "Prison but…" She strokes my head. "We'll think of a way to help him."

"What way?" I ask.

Valentina pauses for the longest time. "I don't know. Yet." She wanders over to the stage and picks up my little sword. She holds it in the sunlight and bounces the reflected sunbeams around the theatre. "I'm going to need to think about it."

Chapter 5

A second later, the side door of the theatre bangs back on its hinges and a man bursts into the sunlight. For the tiniest moment, I think it's Walter, but I'm disappointed. It's Ambrose, another actor.

"Is it true?" he asks the air before seating himself on a shady straw bale and mopping his face with a handkerchief. He arranges his jacket alongside so that it doesn't crease. He pulls out the lace of his cuffs and brushes a mote of dust from his shin. With walnut-stained hair and a painted pointy beard, he's probably the vainest member of the company. He doesn't live here with the rest of us. He has another life, outside.

"At the coffee house this morning, there was talk of a hideous murder down at Welsh Back and, more importantly for us, an arrest. It sounded like Walter!"

"It *was* Walter," says Valentina. "What do you know?"

"Everything I heard is rumour. Blood, tragic death on Welsh Back. First-hand accounts from people who weren't there, the usual guff, but I also heard of connections to our dear queen, and—"

"So Walter's done a murder, eh?" interrupts another voice. It's Bridget. She bustles in through the side door, basket in hand. She also doesn't live in the theatre. She does costumes and says she used to be a leading lady in Bath. A blunt woman, she's got a mushroom nose and grey corkscrew hair that's surrounded by a border of red skin from wearing wigs and make-up. I don't much like her and she doesn't much like me, but we rub along.

"He didn't do it," I say.

Bridget ignores me. "So who did he kill?"

"He didn't," I say again. "It's a mistake."

"Shut up, girl," says Bridget. "I'm trying to find out what's happened."

"As I was going to tell you, this much I know for sure," says Ambrose, rising from his hay bale and running up the stairs on to the stage. "Walter has been arrested by officers of our precious queen for the murder of Lady Margaret Grey!"

Valentina gasps and holds her hands over her mouth.

Another figure appears above us. It's Mrs Hawkin with a basket of shredded undergarments that she begins to arrange on a washing line. The undergarments and Mrs Hawkin have a shared sense of exhaustion and overuse. Watched from below, she pauses and tilts her creaky neck. "Why are you all standing there with your mouths open? What's happened?" she asks.

Ignoring Mrs Hawkin, Bridget asks Ambrose, "And who might Lady Grey be when she's at home? Never heard of her."

"She, my dear Bridget," says Ambrose, stepping daintily towards her, "is — was — a favourite."

"A favourite what?" I ask.

"A favourite to the queen," says Valentina. "It means a close companion. I might have met her once."

"*I* know what it means, Lady Muck," says Bridget, pointing a finger at Valentina. "And of course you've met her. You've met everyone, haven't you."

Valentina narrows her eyes at Bridget, but Bridget ignores her. "But I still don't understand why anyone would murder the queen's favourite in our town. What was she even doing here? It makes no sense at all."

"Just another murder," says Valentina.

"Horrible thing to say," says Bridget.

"Sorry," says Valentina. "But it is."

"Well, if you can't say something nice, say nothing at all," snaps Bridget, pulling a thread out of the hem of her skirt and cutting it with her teeth. "She's a soul lost and that's never a good thing."

Everyone murmurs. I look across at Adam and Eve. They've sneaked down from their quarters and are now sitting opposite me on a bench. Eve sits perfectly still with her hands in her lap. Adam is kicking his toe against the ground. He has a grubby white bandage on his hand. His face is streaked, like he might have been crying. Maybe he's missing Walter too. Or maybe Eve's hurt him. She's always hurting him.

"So what are we to do?" says Mr Hawkin. "One of us is accused of murder. Our reputation is in tatters! But this theatre is our living and our home. Should we keep the lights on in the Moth, our splendid house of entertainment? Stand our ground in the face of adversity and let the storm blow over? Or run for it?" He looks up at the sky. Then down to the ground – and waits.

"We must put it to the vote," says Ambrose. "Personally, I could survive a week without money, but after that…"

"I could take in laundry," says Bridget, staring at her pink hands. "But I'd rather not."

"We should go. Up sticks and move away from here completely. Abandon the Moth. Find another theatre. Another city." Ambrose looks at everyone. "I mean, actors are actors and what's a theatre but a stage and some curtains?"

"We can't do that!" I shout. "We'd be leaving Walter!"

"Shh, child," says Bridget. "This is adult talk."

I think dark thoughts but keep my mouth shut and dig my fingers into Dog's hot fur.

"What do you say, Mrs Hawkin?" asks Mr Hawkin, looking to the gallery. His wife is leaning on the rails. It's hard to imagine, but she was once our leading lady. She passes the back of her hand over her forehead and sighs. "I don't know, Mr Hawkin," she says.

We all look up at her. She's the hardest-working person in this theatre. Not least because she's mother to Eve and Adam and I respect her.

"Birds of one feather," she says in the end.

There's a silence while we all try to understand what she's saying. Mrs Hawkin has a way of talking in proverbs. I don't always see her meaning, but this time I think she's telling us to stick together. I shoot her a tiny smile, and she beams one back.

"Valentina, my dear — what do you think?" asks Mr Hawkin.

"I think," says Valentina, moving to the centre of the stage and kneeling, so that the sunlight falls around her in a pool. "I think…" she pauses until everyone is listening, "that to run would be cowardly, and a betrayal of our comrade, Walter."

Yes!

Now that we're all transfixed, she rises and paces in a small circle. She throws a wide embrace, addressing the empty seats above. "I say we stay and fight; we show our solidarity. We keep the theatre open! We shall not desert our brother!"

"*Oh, brava! Brava!*" says Mr Hawkin, clapping. "*Formidable! Muy, muy bien!* What words, duchess, what words! Now, who votes to leave?"

They look at each other, but none of them vote.

"And to stay?"

It's slow, but they all raise their arms.

"Unanimous!" says Mr Hawkin. "We stay. Onward and upward, troupe. Onward and upward. We have a play to put on. Tonight's performance will be blinding!"

Chapter 6

I want to go and see Walter. I want to go and see where this murder took place, but instead Mrs Hawkin has me polishing shoes and the more I do it, the more furious I feel.

Behind me, Valentina's flapping around with a piece of paper, drawing long elegant letters in ink and tutting when the pen doesn't behave like she wants it to. Her writing's perfect. Just like her dancing and singing and sword fighting. Like me, she's a foundling, but where I was rescued by a boy in a theatre, she says she was found by wolves in a forest. One of those wolves took her to a castle, to a duchess. The duchess decided to keep this strange, red-haired, silver-eyed feral baby, driving away her wolfish ways and replacing them with dancing and languages and beautiful handwriting. But sometimes, although in every sense a duchess, Valentina is still wild, and sometimes I can see the wolves in her eyes.

Like now.

"What am I going to do to help Walter, Valentina?"

She pulls my hair into a ponytail and swooshes it across her cheeks like a powder brush. "I've been thinking about that. Remember when I went away last year?"

I nod. Valentina missed a whole winter season. She went back to the duchess in her castle in the forest, where someone was ill and had called for Valentina. (Without her, Mrs Hawkin had to play Juliet to Walter's Romeo. The audience thought it was hilarious.) When she came back, Valentina had money to spend and freckles on her cheeks.

She bounces the ponytail on my nose. "While I was travelling, I met some very important people, and one of them was a sea captain. I've written him a letter — you could deliver it for me."

"He's here?"

"Yes, amazingly his ship is moored on Narrow Quay this month." Her smile stretches right across her face. Warm and reassuring.

"Why would he help Walter?"

"He likes me. And he's a..." she hesitates. "A moral man. A truth-seeker. He'd want to see the right person convicted." She hands me the boat's name scribbled on the corner of an old script. "It's right down the end of the quay at the moment. A big old ship. You'll know it when you get there."

"You could go. Mrs H has got me cleaning shoes," I say.

"Oh, I would, but I have so much to do without Walter here. There's a whole play to rewrite before tonight. Anyway, she won't mind – Mrs H is just giving you something to do. Something to fill your head so that you don't dwell on Walter. Taking this letter would actually be helpful." She twists her neck and looks at me down her eyelashes. Hooking my arm in hers and pulling me tight so that I'm caught in her warmth and perfume.

"If you really think so."

"I've got the letter here." She waves the paper at me, and although it's folded over, I can see her signature. Looking sideways at it, as if it's a drawing, she dips her quill in the ink and writes a name, tracing a long flourish around it that reaches to the bottom of the page. She sprinkles sand on the ink and props a stick of sealing wax against the candle to warm. "If you popped over now, you'd be back in plenty of time for the performance. They're still arguing about who should do what. You've got hours."

"Should I go in disguise?"

She laughs. "Of course. Always a good idea to be someone else. Take every opportunity to pretend." She pops some rose petals inside, drips the wax on to the letter and seals it. Finally she puffs perfume over it and blows it a kiss. "There," she says, handing it to me.

On the front it says: *Captain Teach. The Running Stag*

In the distance a clock strikes. She's right, we've got ages until we go on stage. Without Walter, it's plain that we can't do what we were doing before. Valentina will make changes to the script, and we'll probably fall back on the murder play. They loved it last time around. And there are posters all over town telling them we're doing a tragedy. We can't suddenly do a comedy. They'll kill us.

Or at least they'll throw things at us.

"Shall I be a boy?"

"Why not?" she says, and she reaches for a boy's cap from the teetering pile of mouldy hats. "An errand Mouse," she giggles.

Chapter 7

By the main door of the theatre, I squeeze past Kwadwo. He's swept the floor and there are hot food smells floating from his cavern by the stage. Right now he's repainting a backdrop. The scenery leaning on the side of the stage has palm trees and he's touching up the long teeth on a huge animal where the paint has cracked. He's concentrating so hard, the tip of his tongue is poking out between his lips, and his nose is practically touching the canvas. I watch him work. He's so skilled. Each brushstroke brings the animal to life.

Kwadwo is our secret weapon. No one outside the

theatre knows who he is; no one knows who paints our scenery, or fills the theatre with the right perfumes for each play. They don't know how it happens, they just know that the Moth is magical. So magical that our audience comes from far and wide.

He's only here because of the fates. As a small child he was taken from Africa to the New World and on the ship his mother died. The captain of the ship thought he was pretty, brought him here to our town and he grew up to speak perfect English, paint pictures and act as a house servant and cook. They gave him the name Caesar Africanus, but they didn't give him anything else. He lived under the captain's house and rarely saw the daylight. One sunny day, when he was fourteen and I was five, he couldn't bear it any more and ran away to hide in the docks, planning to join a pirate ship and go to sea, but Mrs Hawkin found him searching through the rubbish by the river. She brought him in, fed him and eventually he told her his real name, Kwadwo. The company welcomed him and he began his third life in the theatre as a cook and set builder. He's been here ever since. Hiding.

Finally he notices me watching. "Ah, Mouse, I wanted you. You on your way somewhere?"

I nod.

"With Dog?"

I nod again.

"Wait there." "He disappears back into his fragrant lair and comes out carrying a basket covered in a cloth. He's wearing a thick blanket over his head and shoulders.

"I need to take this to Walter," he says.

"But you can't go out now – in broad daylight," I say. "Even wearing that lot over your head. You'll be recognised."

He frowns. "They don't feed them in there. Only crusts and water if he's lucky. And he won't be."

"Walter doesn't get fed?"

Kwadwo shakes his head and pulls a theatrically sad face. "Mouse, sometimes you're too innocent."

"He'll starve!" I say, taking hold of the handle of the basket and stuffing the letter under my jacket.

"No, I should do it, I just wanted you to come—"

"No, *I'll* take it. It's mid-morning. I've got Dog. You can't risk it."

Without giving him a chance to argue I step out of the front of the theatre into the sun.

Immediately I wish I was wearing something thinner. It's hot. Mid-September hot. The shadows are longer, but the ground has heated up all summer. The mud that always forms outside the theatre is crusted in ruts. Dog immediately snuffles off to find something disgusting embedded in a pothole.

"Dog!" I say. "Dog – don't! Don't eat it."

He flicks a guilty gaze at me and crunches something hard between his teeth. Shards of black and bone fall to the ground and he picks at more.

This is where the audience gathers each night before our performances, and the ground gets poached by their feet and littered with food scraps and stinking things.

From the sea of mud the theatre rises four storeys into the sky. It's circular and wooden; the bottom half pinned with posters held on by rusty tacks. Above that, silvered timber, patchworked with repairs. Cut into the top storey is a band of small windows. Some of them have glass; some of them are only there for the winds and the birds. On the very top, above the strip of thatched roof that rings the walls, flaps a small embroidered flag that tatters itself in the wind. It has a moth on it, but age has made it faint. At the bottom of the theatre, over the main door is a large carved moth that Kwadwo made some summers ago. I remember it being vibrant pinks and greens, but now it's soft and brown.

Everything about the theatre is worn. Everything has seen a better life. But this is my magical home and I love it here. Although – is it home without Walter?

I push the idea away. Walter will be back soon. It's all just a terrible mistake. Valentina's sea captain will help. By tomorrow, Walter'll be home, I'm sure of it.

Chapter 8

I take off my jacket and sling it over my shoulder. Set back from the theatre are warehouses of every size and age. They all have their own smells. Coffee, wool, spices, apples, tar. There's also sugar that the ships bring in. There are five sugar houses here, cooking up the brown liquid that comes from the New World in barrels and turning it into white crystals that ladies put in their tea. Cooking the sugar stinks. Sometimes it's delicious, almost chocolatey, and sometimes it catches on fire and the sugar boils out of the doorways.

Kwadwo buys supplies from all of the warehouses but from one in particular. It sells a kind of oil that he uses in his cooking and it smells heavenly. He says it's made of a fruit called an olive. I don't know what olives are but I wish I did.

Behind the warehouses, and at the back of the theatre, are the docks. Huge ships with tree-trunk masts bob in the scummy water, rising and falling on the tide. Now, at high tide, men are loading from the quaysides. They've taken off the barrels of sugar and are replacing them with bales of wool. Kicking them, hoisting, shouting all day long. Their end-of-summer skins are varying shades of red and brown and they sing as they work. Also, the end-of-summer rat population is at its fattest and the activity around the ships is sending the rats into frenzies along the cobbles and between patient horses' feet.

Dog takes off after a particularly swollen one and I hear its quick death take place behind some barrels.

"That's one less," laughs a man pushing a cart.

I weave through the people, the bonfires, the ropes, the noise and dive off into the houses on the far side of the bridge. Their fronts face the roads behind, their backs the harbour. That's why all the quays are called "Backs" here. Welsh Back is where all the Welsh cargo arrives, coal and slates and cockles. The houses are where the merchants live and they seem to spend all day arguing with each other, shouting and doing deals.

None of them notice me, my dog and my basket.

Basket.

I should drop that off first.

But I could just go and see where the murder happened. Perhaps I can find out if there was a witness.

It's only just down the quay to my left.

I whistle and Dog trots close to my heel as we wind past the sailors to the Backs at the end. There's a strong smell of fish left behind from the morning markets. Only thunderstorms and winter storms ever get rid of it.

I stop, uncertain where to look. This is Welsh Back, but where was the murder? There's a huge expanse of cobbled paving sloping towards the water. Without a hope of spotting anything helpful, I wander back and forth over the stones, examining the ground. If the blood on Walter is anything to go by, there'll be plenty here somewhere.

I come upon a pile of wet sawdust, stained red. I stop.

Is that all there is to mark the place where she died?

I look around. Sailors are running back and forth, busy people with busy lives. No one seems to care.

Dog and I stand by the sawdust for a moment, and I feel sad.

"Woman stabbed there this morning," says a girl

scuttling past lugging a handcart loaded with milk churns.

"Did you see anything?" I ask.

She shakes her head. "Did you? They're asking for witnesses."

"No. Are there any witnesses so far?"

"Won't know till tomorrow – they'll put up a poster later on tonight. It'll say everything they know and the things they want to know."

"Where?" I say as she gives her cart a kick to get it moving.

She shrugs. "Here somewhere. They do it every time someone gets murdered."

I watch her pulling and pushing the heavy cart, milk sloshing from the top, heading for the ships.

"We should do something, Dog," I say. "Leave something to mark the place."

He looks up at me and I look up at our surroundings. Behind us is the tall wall of a garden. At the very top, falling in looped tresses, are swags of honeysuckle. I stand underneath, breathing in the blossom. It almost conquers the smell of fish. Reaching up, I snap off three short sprays and, plaiting their stems together, lay them on the pile of sawdust and stand for a moment in memory of a woman I've never met.

A minute later, I turn away. It feels better.

I veer back and head for the Shambles meat market where, between the hanging carcasses of hares and sheep and pigs, people and carts shove this way and that. Sharp flesh smells turn my stomach and I remember that I haven't eaten. A boy's standing on the side with a basket of fruit buns. I nearly buy one but then I spot the pool of animal blood lapping at the bottom. We pass a woman selling eggs and I have a sudden memory of Kwadwo and Walter feeding me eggs. Eggs with runny yolks. I didn't have the words to explain that to me the runny middle was disgusting. They tried again and again with the eggs, feeding all the rejected ones to Dog, which made him fart, until Kwadwo gave me a hard-boiled egg. It was delicious, and they danced around in celebration that they'd found what it was I wanted to eat.

The memory catches me out.

We wriggle through the crowd and emerge on the green. The castle is off to my right and the prison is next to it. We peel off into these narrower, quieter streets. Somehow, although the sun's still shining, the streets get darker as we go.

We turn left, right, left and then a tall soot-black wall rears up, doorless, with a grid of gratings scattered higgledy-piggledy. It's the outer wall of the prison and it's dripping. Not rain dripping, seep dripping.

Even through the stone, I can smell sourness. There's no one around and in this busy city it's eerily quiet. I tiptoe along the wall. The pavement slopes downhill and as it slopes, it shows small barred openings at foot level. Dog sniffs at one, and then jumps backwards as grubby hands grasp the bars and an awful howl echoes past my feet.

I leap to the other side of the alley so that I'm well clear of the windows and hide in the deep shadows. My fingers reach for Dog's collar and we stand and observe the black building. Each opening is dark except for the hands reaching out of it. "Child! Child!" shouts a woman at one of the openings. "Come here, pretty child! I could tell your fortune!"

Dog growls, placing himself between me and the prison.

"Walter! I want Walter Stroud!" I shout, and my voice reverberates from the walls. A chorus of baying and whooping fills the air as everyone in the prison replies.

"Mouse! Mouse!" Walter's voice rings out. For a moment I think he's free, he's somewhere near me, but it's coming from a tiny high window. "Mouse!" he shouts again.

I lean back against the wall opposite and Dog barks.

"Walter?" I shout.

"Oh, Mouse, thank the lord. I knew you wouldn't abandon me."

"What happened? Tell me."

"I just saw the woman on the ground. There was so much blood, and then they all came round the corner – chased me all the way to the theatre. But I'm innocent!"

"He's innocent," says a voice. "Course he's innocent."

"Blood! Oooh – he's a murderer! We've got a murderer in our midst!" squeals a voice. "I'm scared!"

Peals of laughter ring out over the alleyway.

"They're looking for witnesses, Walter," I shout back. "I hope there might be one by tomorrow."

"The murderer needs a witness! Anyone?"

They howl again.

"I've got food for you, from Kwadwo!"

"Mouse has food!" bays another voice.

"Mouse!" yell two more until the whole alley is ringing with my name.

"Food! Food! Food!" they chant, and I tighten my grip on the basket handle.

"How do I get it to you, Walter?"

"A line," he says. "Does anyone have a string?"

"I do!" calls a voice.

"I do," another bellows.

"Wait there, Mouse. Don't go!"

"Don't go, Mouse, don't go!" mimics someone.

"Try the gaoler," a woman shouts.

I look towards the gateway of the prison. It doesn't look at all welcoming.

I'm on the verge of walking over when a piece of knotted string swings from one window to another and a hand – Walter's? – grabs it and feeds it down to me. It bounces from the blocks of stone and catches on other people's windows, before stopping a little above my eye level.

I cross the alley and while hands paw my ankles and I resist the impulse to run, I tie the string around the basket handle and stand back. "Go!" I call, and Walter begins to pull. Hands reach from the grilles and grab at thin air. Walter pulls the basket as hard and fast as possible, but fingers mid-way up the wall latch on to the wicker and hold tight.

"Ha!" shouts someone. "I got it."

"Let go, it's mine!" Walter pulls again and the basket begins to tip.

"Stop!" I shout. "You'll lose it all!"

But Walter tugs and the hand grips and the basket turns, tipping all of Kwadwo's beautiful food out and over and down: bowl, bread, stew and vegetables mixing and tumbling, some inside the gratings but most of it into the street below.

A filthy hand reaches out and scoops the broken bowl from the cobbles, and a second later the basket rolls over towards me.

Empty.

"I'm sorry, Walter! I'm sorry!" I shout. "I'll come again tonight. I'll come every night after the play!"

Someone laughs and the whole prison seems to laugh with them. Dog barks and barks and all my resolution fades. I grab the basket and I run away. Faster and faster I race, my feet out of step, my legs burning, my face burning, just getting away, getting as far away as possible.

Chapter 9

Shamefaced and furious, I lead Dog towards the Abbey of St James. It's a still place and I take a moment to breathe and think and drink and wash Kwadwo's basket under a pump. Dog drinks from the puddle below and I sit in the cool shade and try not to dwell on what just happened. The last time I was here in the abbey gardens, there was a fair. It was good for the theatre company; we dressed up in our finery and gave a sample of the play we were doing. There were sideshow marvels: a pig that told fortunes, and a dog with two heads, except it didn't have two heads — one of them was a ball of painted paper strapped to its neck. There was a dancing bear and cockfighting and most of the adults were drunk. Ambrose got very drunk and had to be carried home by Valentina and Mr Hawkin. Walter bought me a black and white felt hat. He told me that one day I would play Pierrette and we waltzed together while a man played a squeeze box. Mr and Mrs Hawkin joined in and danced like young lovers. Later, Eve stole some honeycomb and blamed me. Adam saw it and said nothing.

I wince. It was a happy memory until I remembered that.

With the basket dripping, I set off for Narrow Quay, pulling my cap on to my head and cramming my hair tight inside. I try to imagine myself as someone else. An errand boy from somewhere else. I practise a word or two. "Right, sir, yup. As you say, sir." I change my walk to a swagger, stomping from side to side through the streets. "Got a letta for you. A letta."

I pass the back of a candle shop, where they're rendering carcasses. Choking fatty smoke fills the alley and I have to hold my breath and run, dragging Dog away from a heap of bones shoved to the side. We pop out of the alley, on to Narrow Quay. The ships here are massive. Dwarfing the houses behind them, rammed side by side. At the far right-hand end are two that have died in the harbour, their sides broken, ribs sun-bleached and shattered. I look towards the other end and start reading the names on the biggest of the ships. *The Endurance, The Betty, The Duke, The Concord* and, almost in the open water, *The Running Stag. The Running Stag* isn't like the others. They're all painted, shiny. Shipshape, I suppose. The ship I have to deliver to is silvered, worn. It's the boat equivalent of the Moth and it looks like it's done a lot of voyages. Faded pennants droop from the rigging and the sails are patched. My heart falls as I take in the state of the ship and the only visible member of the crew, an old man slowly scrubbing the deck.

I hope he isn't the captain.

I approach the ship, loitering, waiting, wondering quite how you knock on a ship's door, when a different man sticks his head over the prow and notices me.

"Can I help you?" He's very tall. Broad-shouldered with a neat little black beard. His eyes are bright and dark. He looks like a leading man, like Ambrose wants to look. This must be the captain.

"Brought a letta from Valentina," me-as-errand-boy says. I pull the paper from my jacket pocket. It's crumpled and very slightly wet. It doesn't look anything like as good as it did when Valentina gave it to me.

He clambers down a ladder that reaches up the side

of the ship and takes it from me. Even though I pull my head up from my shoulders and raise my heels from the ground, I still need to tip my head, and I'm left looking past his beard up into his nose.

The rose petals fall to the ground as he reads the letter twice.

He smiles. Something about the letter amuses him. "Does she want a reply?" he says.

I realise that I have no idea. Valentina's instructions didn't go that far. "Er – yup," I say.

"Thank her for the news of the unfortunate man in the prison. Tell her that I will come to the theatre." He stares over my head at the warehouses behind. "Tell her it will all be fine. Got that?"

I nod and turn back among the houses.

It will all be fine?

What does that mean? Does it mean he's going to help get Walter out?

Sometimes I wonder at the people that Valentina knows. But that man was a pirate, or a *privateer*, as they're called.

How on earth would she know someone like that?

When I reach the theatre the midges have risen from the ground and hang in seething clouds over the stage. Mr Hawkin is spraying them with soap from a brass pump that is coating the boards of the stage with slime, making it slippery. Kwadwo has been commandeered to wash it from the boards. The water pools on the sawdust floor below and Kwadwo says that's where the midges lay their eggs. He tries to explain this to Mr Hawkin, but Mr Hawkin has no science in his head. "Only art!" he says, wafting his soap over a wider area.

"Ah — Mouse! Lanterns! Time to light the lanterns! Assist!"

Dog slopes off and I stop to help. Mr Hawkin goes up to the dressing rooms, muttering something about costumes. Ambrose struts down to practise his lines on the empty stage. Abandoning the soap-washing, Kwadwo hands me a lit twist of paper and we fiddle with wicks and candles in the hundreds of mirrored lanterns that the theatre relies on. As everything has been soap-sprayed, including the lanterns, it's all soggy and nothing wants to light. Sooty trails rise from the candle wicks and only a few burn properly.

"How was Walter?" Kwadwo asks when Ambrose throws his script to the floor and turns back to stomp upstairs.

"It was awful," I say. "I—"

I stop. Eve has come out and is watching us from the side of the stage. "You're not very good at this," she says. "I would be much better. If I was doing it, I'd take the lanterns down from the wall and light them all together. Not climb up the ladder each time."

I know this wouldn't work. We've tried it. The lanterns go out if they're moved. Kwadwo shoots me a glance and holds a finger up to his lips. We both stay silent.

Tiring of us, Eve stands and walks off the back of the stage, disappearing up the stairs to the wardrobe rooms.

Mr Hawkin reappears with chairs for the set. "Lord! What's taking you so long?"

"Water, Mr H," I say, willing a damp wick to light. "We're having to light them twice."

"Oh, come on, it's simple. Here – apply flame to candle…" He whisks the spill from my hand and holds it briefly next to a candle wick. "And lo! We have light!" The candle spits and smokes and stays firmly unlit. "Damp – it's damp. Everything in this hellhole is damp!" He hands me the spill. "Keep trying, Mouse, Kwadwo. Keep trying! Onward! Onward!"

The unsoaped midges mill around my head and are joined by early evening moths. At last, between us, Kwadwo and I get the lanterns to burn so that they spill their fractured glow around the galleries and the stage. Their light takes over from the fading day and the theatre assumes its magic, transforming from a heap of rotting timber to the Moth Theatre, a sparkling palace of beauty and greasepaint. Above our heads the golden stars in the heavenly frieze glisten in the candlelight. Under the stage, flames in red glass lanterns flicker to represent the devil's lair. As we light the last few lanterns I tell Kwadwo about the prison and the lost food.

He shakes his head. "Don't worry, Mouse."

"I'll go again – later – after the play."

He turns to look at me. "Really? Walter won't starve overnight."

"There must be a way of getting it to him safely. I think it would be easier in the dark," I lie. "I could try a signal that only he would recognise."

"I'll make the food again. Maybe we should both go."

"No," I say, my voice as confident as I can make it. "You mustn't. And after all, Walter would do it for me, so…"

"We'll talk about it later." He holds my shoulder for a second, his hand warm and comforting. He clambers up on to the stage and crouches to check the floor lanterns.

I watch as he opens the glass doors of the floor lanterns each in turn. Squatting, his legs long and spidery, he folds down to reach the ground. He's a tall, strong man, and I'm me, but I can't let him go to the prison. He only leaves the theatre to go to the warehouses alongside us. And he only does that in the early morning. He never crosses the bridge because of the danger of being recognised by the sea captain who brought him here. Or any of the people that lived in that house. I've asked him about going out at night. He shakes his head and says there are too many people; the early mornings are safest.

I get it, although it was years ago.

He always points to his black skin. "How many of us are there in this town?" he asks.

My skin goes brown in the sun, but not black like his. And he's so tall, so thin, so recognisable. I've lost Walter; I couldn't bear to lose Kwadwo. Going to the prison at night is worth it if I get to keep him.

I climb a stepladder to light the last two lanterns and the first of the stallholders arrives with a basket of sweet bread rolls. "Here, Mouse." He chucks me a saffron bun and I stuff it in my mouth in three bites.

"Thank you," I reply, running back down the ladder.

Outside the big doors I can hear the audience gathering, stamping their feet and calling to each other, and I realise I don't even know what I'll be doing tonight.

Mr Hawkin has vanished into the dressing rooms and when I turn to ask Kwadwo about the food, he's gone.

Chapter 10

Racing up the steps behind the stage, I find the troupe
in chaos. Some of them are learning lines, some trying
on costumes. We're doing a play we've done before but
everyone has moved around the cast list. Bridget and
Ambrose are arguing about the parts they have been
given – or not given.

"But why don't I play Walter's part?" says Ambrose.
"I'm always the villain. It gets tedious, you know. I'd
love to play a leading man."

Mr Hawkin holds up his hands for silence. "As I
said before, Valentina will tie back her hair and be
Walter."

"Why can't you be the leading man, Mr H?" asks Ambrose.

Mr Hawkin shakes his head. We all know he can't because he can't remember the lines, but he won't admit it.

"Or Kwadwo?" mutters Bridget. "He could do it – easy."

Mrs Hawkin shoots her a look. We all know Kwadwo can't, that he's in hiding.

I look across at him. He's soaping Eve's leather harness and won't meet my eye. I wonder if Bridget's being mean because she resents him, or because of the colour of his skin. I suspect he's wondering that too – although sometimes she seems to have it in for all of us.

Mr Hawkin takes a big breath and batters through the conversation. "Mrs Hawkin will be Valentina. Bridget will be Mrs Hawkin. You, Mouse, will play Bridget's parts. Ambrose, you will play the role you played before. And, Kwadwo – you can do all the costume changes and the props – *ut solet.*" Mr Hawkin claps his hands and walks away so that no one can argue with him.

I'm thinking of ways of getting the food to Walter, when Valentina appears. "Here, little one," she says.

"Your costume." She holds out a dress that Bridget wears. It's twice as wide as me. "Hmm – it's a bit big, but we'll pin it," she says, reaching for a pincushion. "What did my sea captain say?"

"He said he was aware of… Well, he called Walter 'unfortunate', so he knows about the arrest. He said he'd come to the theatre but didn't say when. He said to tell you it will be fine. What will be fine? Did you tell him Walter was innocent?"

"Tonight?" Valentina jabs me with a pin.

"OW!"

I rub my side where the pinprick was. "I don't know."

She pokes me with another pin.

"Valentina!" I say.

"What? Spin for me, Mouse."

"Did you tell him Walter was innocent?"

She stops looking at the dress and takes my chin in her hand. Gently, cupping it like I'm her child. "Of *course* I did, poppet." She kisses my forehead.

Feeling a spark of joy in my chest, I whirl for her and she swoops the side of the dress in. "I haven't learned Bridget's lines."

"They're easy, you can make them up. Not the same for me because I'm speaking Walter's words and there are far too many of them." She gives me her warmest smile, the one she doesn't use on stage until the very end of a play. "You'll be fine. I'll be the one covered in egg. Now — do the make-up."

I rush to mix up the pastes that go into the make-up and Mr and Mrs Hawkin arrive at my shoulder, peering into the mortars where I grind up pigments.

"Well, Mrs Hawkin," says Mr Hawkin. "As you will once again be playing our leading lady, you will need a thickish coat of stage paint on that gerontic visage of yours."

She pinches her mouth and swipes the back of his head. His hat flies across the room.

Mr Hawkin strokes his thinning hair. A long strand has escaped and hangs down to his shoulders on one side, and the rest is scraped over his brown-spotted scalp. "*Touché*," he says, sweeping out of the room. "An hour before curtain up! Rally, troops! *En garde!*"

When he leaves, Mrs Hawkin slumps into a chair and struggles to put on her stockings. The skin on her fingers is so rough from endless washing that I can hear it catching on the silk.

"Here, let me help," I say, and I kneel by her feet. She is older than Valentina. Much older. And much more worn. It shows that she's spent a life bent over washing tubs and wrestling with Adam and Eve. Red circles that should be confined to her cheeks spread right across her nose. Hair – once blonde, now silvered – springs wildly over her face and, in the present heat, glues itself to her forehead. Her face is uneven. Her skin lumpy. Her eyes weeping and tired. But she fits into Valentina's green dress. Everything about her is scratchy and I'd love to take some of Valentina's expensive creams and rub them into her poor legs.

Slowly I pull the stockings over her cracked heels.

"Oh, bless you, Mouse," she says, resting a hand on my head. "Reap as you shall sow, my dear father used to say. All the work you put into this life will be rewarded in the next."

"Is that right, Mrs H?" I get the first stocking up to her knee and start on the other. I can't help feeling Mrs Hawkin could do with more rewards in this life rather than waiting for the next one.

"You are a sweetheart," she says, kissing the top of my head. "Now, get on with that make-up. Or we'll all be late to make fools of ourselves."

As Mrs Hawkin rises, her legs in their jaunty orange stockings, Eve brushes past us. She's carrying a pair of wings, and the tip of one catches on a beam and flicks back in my face.

"Ow!"

"Oh – Mouse – sorreeeee," she says.

From the shadows, her mother observes, her mouth falling to a disappointed line.

I hear them have words. Mrs Hawkin's voice soft and placatory. Eve's sharp and hard.

Ignoring their conversation, I grind white lead and blend it with rice powder, pressing it down and round. The gloop in the mortar is starting to form a fine paste.

Perhaps I should have asked the captain straight out, instead of giving him Valentina's letter. He might need more information before he can do anything. It would be really good to have a proper conversation with Walter. Maybe I could go into the prison. Talk to him without all the scary people hanging from the windows.

Dipping my finger in the paste, I can see that it would be fine for Valentina but not Mrs H. I need to thicken it.

Ambrose appears beside me to peer in a mirror. Close up, I can see the white roots of his hair. He sees me looking.

"Make-up covers so many things, Mouse," he says. "Enjoy your youth, sweetheart. Enjoy those somersaults and backflips. One sudden day, they'll desert you and you'll be an old thing like me."

"You're not that old, Ambrose," I say.

"You're very kind, Mouse." He bows and turns away to try on jackets. All the ones he chooses are ever so slightly too tight.

I turn back to my grinding. Make-up does cover so many things but I don't think this one's going to cover Mrs Hawkin's face. I poke into bottles and boxes for something to make the make-up opaque.

"What are you looking for?" Eve sidles up beside me, sweet and wide eyed – her mother's telling-off apparently forgotten.

"Nothing."

"No – go on. I can help."

"Something thick to put in the make-up. It won't cover your ma's cheeks properly – see?" I smear some on the back of my hand.

"No, that won't do at all. She'll look a shock with that on her face and we can't have that. Poor Ma." Eve wanders off towards the paints that Kwadwo uses on the painted heavens, picking up and dropping boxes and jars.

I continue to grind the powders, adding a spot of oil from time to time to try and get something more pasty. My mind wanders back to Walter. I'll try and find out about witnesses tomorrow.

I add a load of chalk and the make-up goes crumbly and billows out of the bowl.

"Ooh – yuck!" says Eve. "You could always try adding some of this." She places a carton on the table next to me. "It'll thicken it. You're going to need something very thick to put on that." She points at her ragged mother, who is cramming her feet into Valentina's dainty boots.

"What is it?"

"White stuff. It's good, it'll cover the ... blemishes. But you'll need lots!" Eve giggles and wafts away to put on her grubby white dress. She almost always dangles innocently above the stage, waving her arms around and making the audience ooh and ahh like she was some kind of angel. Personally, I'd dress her as a bat. Or a small demon. She'd make an excellent fork-wielding little devil, dancing under the stage through the lantern fires of Hell.

I unpack the carton and sniff it. It smells mouldy but not poisonous and I shake some in. Big white crystals clump in the bowl, and I grind them into the powder. They mix quite well so I shake in some more, blend it round, add a dab of amber oil and some water. It seems to fizz a little and then stops. I stir it and stir it and try a little smeared on my brown arms. It covers my skin. With any luck it'll cover the blotches on Mrs H's face.

I look at Eve, who is prancing about in a pair of

raggedy wings. She wouldn't normally do anything to help me.

Perhaps this time she listened when her mother told her to be nice.

Chapter 11

The audience is raucous and shouty.

"Where's the murderer then?"

"Blood and guts, we want blood and guts!"

Poor Mrs Hawkin has to strain to get her words over. They're delighted. Loving every second of the swapped parts. They roar with laughter when Mrs Hawkin puckers her mouth for a kiss with Valentina. They hoot when Valentina, dressed as a man, skips towards her, landing her sweetheart lips on Mrs Hawkin's painted mouth.

They go wild for Ambrose. Even more than usual.

"More! More!" they yowl as we come off for the interval.

"That was all right," says Valentina, pulling the belt tighter around her waist to keep Walter's trousers from falling down. "We didn't even make that many mistakes."

"My face," mutters Mrs Hawkin, bustling over to the mirror and slapping more of the thick white paste over her ruddy cheeks. "Itching."

"Help me with my wings, Mouse," says Eve. "They're slipping." She holds up her arms and waits.

I tighten the harness on her wings and they rise up her back until she looks like an angel again.

Mrs Hawkin scratches her face. "It's burning," she says, peering at herself. "What's wrong with me?"

"Time to get back on stage," says Mr Hawkin. "Two minutes, everyone."

We stumble through the second half. Catcalls and wolf whistles accompany Mrs Hawkin every time she speaks and it's almost impossible to hear anything she says.

I wait in the wings. Adam waits next to me. He winces as his mother's wig slips and a roar rises from the crowd. "Oh no," he says. "Poor Ma."

"You're on!" hisses Mr Hawkin, and I trot forward to stand in the middle of the stage.

"My lord," I say, and my mind goes blank. "My lord..."

"Your wife awaits!" comes a whisper from behind. I glance back. It's Adam. I hesitate. Can I trust him?

"Come on!" shouts someone from the crowd.

"Get on with it!" yells another.

"Your wife awaits," I say, and Mrs Hawkin stumbles out from behind me to a cascade of laughter.

I say another line, but no one could possibly hear it. We stagger on.

A two-hour play takes three hours and I'm exhausted by the time we reach the end but I'm ready to go to the prison again. The moment I can, I rush off stage and glance back to see Valentina centre stage, taking her bow. The audience thump and shout and whoop. She bows again and a small boy runs up to the stage and hands her a tiny yellow bird in a cage.

"Oooo-ooooh!" choruses the crowd.

Valentina picks up the cage and peers at the bird. I don't think I've ever seen her look so happy. She blows an elegant kiss to someone in the gallery. I follow her gaze but it's too full and too noisy.

She comes off stage clutching the cage and dances up the stairs, her smile filling her whole face.

"Who's it from?" I ask, following her.

"You know, the captain. Captain Teach," she giggles.

"Your fancy man? Another sucker beguiled by the wolf tale?" asks Bridget, hoisting herself up the stairs behind us. "Giving you birds, eh?"

Valentina throws herself full length on a pile of coats, and wriggles. She rests the cage on her chest. "My own little songbird!" she laughs. "I've always wanted one!"

Bridget loosens the strings that are holding her together. "Birds in cages? Not nice in my view."

Valentina rolls on to her back and pokes at the little bird through the bars with the long nail on her little finger. The bird hops on and off the tiny perch and twitters.

I turn away. For some reason it's making me uncomfortable.

Chapter 12

I'd ask Valentina more about the captain, but she's too obsessed with her new toy and she's gone with it into her sleeping space. As it is, I need to go to the prison.

While I'm pulling on a dark-brown jacket, there's a commotion behind me. It's Mrs Hawkin, and she's in tears.

"Ow, ow!" she howls, splashing her face with water. "What is this? Why does it hurt so much?"

"What ails you, my sweet?" says Mr H.

"My face, my face — it's on fire!"

"Oh my lord — look at her!" says Bridget. "She's beetroot!"

"Hold on, let me assist," says Mr H, dabbing at his wife's face with a handkerchief.

"That's useless." Bridget brushes him away. "We need a bucket of water and a mop. Who mixed up the make-up?"

"I did. Why?"

"What did you put in it, child?" asks Mr Hawkin.

"The usual – chalk and rice powder and white lead. And this stuff." I reach for the box of white crystals. "I was trying to make it thicker."

"That? You used that?" Mr Hawkin rolls his eyes and holds the carton at arm's length. "That's soda ash. They're cleaning crystals."

"I didn't know. Eve told me to—"

"No, I didn't!" says Eve, who has Adam hard at work unstrapping her wings. "You're lying!"

"Yes, you did!" I snap.

"Did you tell her to use it?" Mr Hawkin asks his daughter.

"No, of course not, Pa. I wouldn't dream of it. It was going to go on poor Mama's lovely face. She's got it completely wrong." Eve's still wearing her halo. She looks like a vision of virtue, and she's doing the tiptoe thing she does on stage that makes her seem to float above the ground. She glances over to Valentina as if she wants her to watch this performance, but

Valentina is studying her script. Eve pulls her mouth into a sweet smile. Tilts her head. "I love you, Mama," she says, with a kiss on her lips. "I'm sorry that horrible Mouse has made you so red and boily."

I open my mouth, and close it again. There's no point in saying or trying or anything. I have fallen into one of Eve's traps.

"You wretched child!" shouts Bridget, grabbing a broom and waving it at me. "You imbecile. What possessed you? What are we going to do tomorrow? Eh? She can't go on stage again like this."

I risk a glance at Mrs Hawkin. She's managed to get some of the paste off, but her face is now redder and rawer than before. And she's crying. "My skin's on fire – I've never felt such pain."

"See what you've done!" says Bridget. "Ruined her. She's utterly ruined!" She casts her voice into the rafters and cries "Ruined!" for a third time. "I shall have to play the part tomorrow. She can't possibly!"

I start to speak, but Ambrose passes and puts his fingers up to cover my lips. "Stay quiet, Mouse. Anything you say will just fan the flames. It'll blow over."

While the company flock around Mrs Hawkin, dabbing at her and suggesting things that might work on her skin, Kwadwo appears, carrying a green plant. It's made from fat juice-filled spikes. I've seen it growing on his windowsill. "Here, Mrs H," he says, snapping a point from the plant and holding it by a candle's light until a clear bubble appears. He hands it to her. "Aloe. It'll ease the burn. It'll mend you soon enough. Rub this end on your face."

Mrs Hawkin eyes the plant and smears the thick green stem on her skin. It leaves a snail trail of silver. "It's just sap, leave it on there," says Kwadwo. He touches my arm. "Are you still able to go to Walter?"

I nod.

He opens his mouth to say something but Mr Hawkin grabs me by the elbow. "Get rid of this stuff, Mouse," he sighs. "And grow some sense."

I run down the back stairs to the street, raging, imagining Eve in a pit of vipers but feeling such a fool for being distracted. I should have known she'd never suggest anything helpful – she must have seen Mrs Hawkin kiss my head and been jealous. This way she's managed to get both of us.

I spoon the white mixture out into the gutter.

"Stupid," I say to myself. "Stupid."

"Yes – glad you understand it at last," says Eve, dogging my steps. "You always were an idiot." She watches me struggle with the white paste. "Almost no fun. Too easy." She turns to go upstairs. "I don't know what they see in you."

Her brother appears at the bottom of the stairs. "Come up, Eve. Leave Mouse alone."

Eve looks at her brother and pokes him in the ribs. "Not sympathising with the enemy, are you?"

Adam kicks his toe against the wall. He doesn't look at me. "She's beneath you," he mutters. "Not worth the effort. Come and see poor Ma. Her face is very pink."

"Prettier than usual then," says Eve, letting out a horrible snarly laugh. "Come on, brother dear, I'm bored of Mouse-baiting. Let's find something else to play with."

Chapter 13

My anger boils up and simmers down and I stand looking at the sky while a fine summer rain begins to fall. It washes my face, taking away the heat, so that when Kwadwo comes to find me with his basket once again laden with food, I'm almost recovered.

As we stand in the shadows, I can hear him breathing in the cool damp air. "Mouse? Are you sure about this? I could still come too."

"Yes," I lie. "Quite sure. I hope Walter still has his piece of string from earlier."

"I've given you my catapult, a stone and a line, just in case. Have you worked out a signal?"

I nod.

"I owe you, Mouse," he says.

"You know I'd do it anyway."

Dog sniffs the air and I lodge the basket in the crook of my arm. We set off at a jog over the softening mud and weave between the quiet warehouses towards the city bridge.

On the other side the streets are dark and glisten in the rain but in this city that never goes quiet there are people and animals out here scuttling, flicking between the shadowed doorways. Following Dog, who seems to know where we're going, I head down Wine Street where the drunks are collecting at the sides and the really drunk are already insensible in the gutters.

Ahead of us, three boys are baiting a dog with a stick. Dog pauses as if he wants to help the other dog but I pull him away. I know those boys. They're thieves. They haven't learned to cut throats yet, but they're nasty.

No one calls or reaches for us and we keep running. Dog takes a turn but with a low whistle I call him back to me and we enter the final filthy alley where the prison stands.

Darkness. Total darkness.

I puff out a couple of times as if my legs were

going to run again and swallow down the panic that's forming imaginary monsters in every velvet shadow. Ahead of me the wall of the prison rears up against the star-spotted sky. Dog growls.

"Shh, Dog," I breathe, staring into the darkness until I can make out the shapes of the windows. They are mostly slightly paler, so there must be candles in some of the cells. Some of them gape a deeper, darker black than the sooty walls.

Counting from the right, I focus on the one I think Walter must be in. Directly below it is a line of windows. That would make sense. At the very bottom is a grating at foot level. I tiptoe forward and run my toes over the cobbles. Something sticky catches on the sole of my boot. Could it be the remains of Kwadwo's stew?

Stepping backwards again, I line up the windows.

That one at the top has to be Walter's.

"*I'll sing you one, O.*" The notes fall dead in the air. Too quiet.

I wait. There's no answer.

"*Green grow the rushes, O.*" This time I let the sound roll, but there's still no answer.

Crouching, I let my fingers trawl the ground until I find a tiny pebble.

I fit it into the leathery strip that stretches from

the catapult.

I can do this, says the voice in my head. But I can't even see the Y of the catapult, I can only feel it in my hand and I've never really used it. I steady it with my thumb and point it up towards the prison walls. Pulling the leather strip back I feel it springing, and then I release.

I hear the pebble strike at the top of the wall somewhere and clatter down. I think it was too high.

I try another. It disappears without any sound. Perhaps it went in? I pick another tiny pebble from the ground. My eyes are getting used to the dark now and I can actually see this little stone right up to the moment at which it disappears into what I hope is the right window.

I'm about to risk all and send Kwadwo's larger pebble wrapped in string flying through the air, when I hear something.

"One is one and all alone and evermore shall be so."

"Walter?" I breathe.

"Mouse?" A whisper no louder than the wind.

Something white and straight descends. I step forward and fumble with knots, fastening the basket tight.

I tug on the line.

He tugs back and the basket rises, a blob of pale

in the black.

A moment later the basket flies over my head and bounces on the cobbles behind me.

"What's 'at?" says a voice.

"Someone there?" shouts another.

Dog and I turn away. "We did it!" I yelp.

Dog yaps and bounds off along the narrow streets and I follow, racing all the way back to the theatre.

Chapter 14

When we return, the candles are guttering and the theatre has an exhausted air. Upstairs among the costume racks I find Mrs Hawkin, who is still daubing her face with silver slime from Kwadwo's plant. She's sitting, gazing at her reflection in a smeary mirror. Red eyes. Red skin.

"I'm sorry," I say as I pass her on my way up to my eyrie at the top of the theatre. "I didn't know what it was. I wouldn't have used it if I'd been thinking properly."

She reaches for my wrist as I pass. "It's all right, Mouse. I didn't think for one minute that you did it on purpose. I know you're a good child. You've a kind heart. You're my little Mouse Heart." She puts the scrap of Kwadwo's plant on the table. "It was the green-eyed god that did it. My daughter's awful jealousy. Still, it's better to be envied than pitied, hold that in your heart." She pulls me against her chest for a second. Just as she would when I was small and Adam and I shared her lap.

"Thank you, Mrs H," I say to her chin.

"Have you been out?"

I nod.

"To see poor Walter?"

"Yes. But Valentina has a plan to help him."

She's silent for a long time. Then she says, "Take care, little one. 'Tis a bold mouse that nestles in the cat's ear." She waggles my nose and pushes me away.

"Oh?"

But she gets up and walks off down the stairs to her family's quarters, leaving me to blow out the lanterns in the costume room. What did she mean by that?

"You all right, Mouse?" comes a voice from the dark as I rustle my way through the costume store. Valentina.

At night, the theatre spaces convert to sleeping quarters. We all have little cubby holes. Valentina's is in a bay at the back of the costume store. She says it's like the stern of a galleon; makes her feel like she's on the sea. Mine's up in the eaves above her. We're the only two in the dressing room; everyone is scattered all over the building. The Hawkins have a curved room that uses half the gallery. Walter's is above the scenery-painting studio. Kwadwo sleeps at the bottom, in the scenery store. His own world of painted elephants and palaces.

"I delivered food to Walter."

"That's good, but poor Walter," says Valentina.

I hear her open the window above her bed. Her bird is still twittering.

"Shhh!" she says. "Be quiet, little thing."

"I think you have to cover them," I say. "Then they go to sleep."

She rustles something and then asks, "Are you miserable?"

"Yes," I say quietly.

"You need to think of something cheerful – something to give you happy dreams. I know – I'll tell you a story. Did I ever tell you about the kitchen boy in the castle and the rattling spider caught in the cooking pot that scared us for a whole night?"

"Yes," I say. "Twice."

"Oh, I'll think of another one. I know: Mrs Hawkin used to be married to a rich man and left him to live with Mr Hawkin – all for love. Isn't that sweet? Oh, and did you know that you're so much cleverer, more talented and graceful than Eve – always, poppet. You always are, you always have been."

"Thank you," I murmur.

"One more thing," she says. "You might get to perform for a queen!"

"What – here?"

"Yes! Apparently her palaces in London are too hot so she's coming down for a month. A whole month!"

"To the Moth?" I ask.

"Possibly," she says. "But don't tell anyone until I'm absolutely sure. Night, Mouse. Sleep well."

"Night, Valentina," I say, and taking the last of the lanterns I climb on the hampers to reach my tiny space above the rafters.

The queen? Here? Mr Hawkin will explode when he hears that. He'll be unbearable.

I hope we've got Walter back by then.

Broad beams that hold the roof together cross an arm's length above my head. Dog settles on my feet and I reach up to the lower of the huge pieces of timber.

My fingers run over the carvings I've done there over the years. Walter, Dog, Kwadwo, Valentina, Mrs Hawkin, Mr Hawkin, Adam, Eve. Last time Eve caught me in one of her traps, I carved wings on either side of her dress and then added two horns to her head. I must have been even angrier back then.

This time I take my knife and score a heart to surround Walter and continue carving until my bed is covered in tiny shavings.

Finally, when I'm almost happy with it, my candle dies. In the dark, I press my palm against the carvings. Walter's heart is deep in the grain of the beam.

Exhausted, I collapse back on to the pillow and cry.

Chapter 15

I dream of Walter, that he's here, right beside me, and when I wake to find Dog instead I remember what that milk girl said yesterday: that they'd put a poster up about witnesses. I need to go and take a look.

Grabbing my boots, I slip downstairs past Valentina, who is fast asleep, and her bird, who is not. It's just past seven and the day's already heating up. Dog trots at my heels and I meet Kwadwo returning from the warehouses clutching a bag of apples.

"Where are you going?" he asks.

"Just out," I say.

He throws me an apple and I munch it as I walk.

I'm not going to tell Kwadwo what I'm doing. He'd be worried. I don't want to do that to him. I want to keep him safe, like he and Walter always did for me.

On the other side of the bridge, the boats are already leaving on the tide. One after another they drift from their moorings and the sailors pole them downstream towards the sea. Crying women and bewildered children wave coloured clothes at the departing ships and I weave my way through until I'm on the Backs.

There's no sign now of where the woman died.

Yesterday's pile of sawdust has gone.

So where would they put a poster up? Dog sniffs at the ropes and finds something dead to eat and I wander the walls, all of them plastered with notices. So many of them, but none to do with the murder. Perhaps I'm too soon? Or too late? I keep going until I reach the last wall. It's a wooden stockade held together by the paper. Most of them are our playbills faded and out of date. But there's one, right in the centre. Freshly pasted. The milk girl was right.

Murder most horrid

On Thursday 10th September, struck down in daylight, Lady Margaret Grey, handmaid to Her Majesty the Queen. Though she fought for her life, her assailant was strong and persistent. The last of her life left her before she could identify her attacker. There is one witness. His testimony is that he saw a man flee from the scene. Although we have a person of interest in custody, we would prefer further witness for a swift conviction. Should you have information please come forward to Her Majesty's Officers, Messrs Jameson and Stuart at the White Lion.

A witness?

"A witness, Dog!"

If there's a witness, then surely Walter will be freed. Unless the witness identified Walter as the murderer. But they wouldn't, because he didn't do it.

I read the poster again.

Jameson and Stuart at the White Lion. Those two! The ones who took Walter away and called me a nothing. But the White Lion is nearby.

Dog falls into step and we head over the cobbles towards the new square. Tall crisp houses rise from fresh earth, wooden scaffolding still covering the fronts. Glassless windows blink in the light and doorless doorways gape, but behind them is an old stone inn, leaning as if squashed by a giant foot. A steady stream of fishmongers from the early market are already drinking, coming and going, carrying morning flagons of cider, and I watch to see if there's any sign of the two men who took Walter.

I'd go inside, but how to do it without being recognised?

I look down. I'm wearing different clothes to yesterday. Could I be a pirate boy? Picking up a mangy piece of string, I plait my hair into a single long rope and tuck it inside my collar. I pull up the collar so that it surrounds my chin and roll up the bottoms of my trousers, leaving a gap between them and my boots. I pull a twig from a bush and chew some of it off, so that there's a dark blob of bark to stick over my teeth. Pirates have terrible teeth.

I take a red handkerchief from my pocket and knot it around my neck.

Last, I tie Dog to a post sticking out of the cobbles.

He lets out a groan of protest. "I'm sorry," I say. "I know this is mean but you can't come with me."

He settles on his stomach and lets his head fall on his forepaws, sulking.

Making my steps small and unsteady, I push up through the people around the doorway inside the inn. It's not full, which is a shame, as it makes it harder to blend in. There are people standing, talking, drinking, but no one I recognise. I walk straight through to the back and stop in a little passage between two halves of the building.

Now what?

I can't loiter here, can I?

A man brushes past to the yard at the back and I suddenly find something really interesting to look at on the floor. Crouching, I tie and untie my shoelaces, doing it as if I've only recently learned and making it go wrong, twice.

As I fiddle, I look up, just a little. On my left is a room with a fireplace and half a dozen tables. There are men in there, talking. I risk a longer stare. Yes! Jameson and Stuart are sitting at the back. Both of them have their feet on a pile of firewood and, even better, their backs to me.

I slip inside and crouch halfway under a table. I fiddle with my bootlaces again and keep my nose pointing at the ground.

They're talking about a duke from the continent. How he's got spies in every town. How he's rumoured to have employed an assassin to kill the queen but their conversation is going around in circles. Then they talk about a woman who works for the queen who might or might not be a double agent, then another spy found dead in a ditch. They talk so long, my leg goes to sleep and I have to swap sides. Finally one of them says, "So where we at with Margaret

Grey's murder then?"

There's a long sigh, a fart and someone rustles some paper.

A man comes in with a flagon of ale and sits at the table I'm hiding under. I edge away from him and a second man comes to sit down. I'm stuck between their feet. They start talking to each other so I have to strain to listen to Jameson and Stuart, who are far quieter.

"Well, the actor's in the gaol, but now we've got a witness says it's not him," says Jameson.

"That is very inconvenient – all the evidence points to him." Stuart pauses, and when he starts talking again, he's muffled. Like he's chewing something. "He was covered in blood. Could a stray witness be ignored?" He swallows. "Or as Queen's Officers do we have to do it like we're s'posed to?"

There's a long silence and I wonder if they're going to say anything else. Someone in the room knocks something liquid over and I hear water trickle to a stone floor.

"I don't know," Jameson sighs. "She was a royal agent. Very close to Her Majesty, by all accounts. We'll get caught out if we don't tell something close to the truth. I'll go and talk to him. I'll go tomorrow."

"Who?"

"Dale, the bootman — he's our witness. The only one."

One of the men at my table stands, and I back slowly from the room, still crouching, until I'm well clear.

Chapter 16

It takes me seconds to run back through the inn, grab Dog and pull my hair out of the string. As casually as I can, I wander along the quayside, restored to myself, thinking.

"A witness, Dog. We've got a witness. Mr Dale."

Dog is unmoved, but my heart's singing. I know Mr Dale. He comes to the theatre from time to time. He's a kind man. He sometimes pays for paupers to see the plays.

The alley to my left leads towards the town. Towards the boot shop. I'll go now before Jameson does.

I jog through the lanes until I can see the row of

tatty shops that houses the boot-mender's. There's no one waiting and the door stands open. I cross the road, dodging carts and people on horseback, and stop outside the shop. It's lit by a dim lantern. The smell of leather and neat's-foot oil fights with boiling rabbit glue and stinking feet. In the far corner, Mr Dale is bent over an anvil, bouncing a leather hammer off the sole of a boot. The place rings with the thumping and I have to wait for him to stop before I can say anything. While I'm standing there, I study his workshop. Unfolded shoes and curled boot soles lie in heaps on the floor. Tall stacks of paste and jars of browns, every shade from chestnut to ebony. How does he ever find anything?

On one side of the workshop a set of stairs leads up; on the other, a door opens into a brewery yard. Out there the sun's blinding, lighting every bobble of beer as it foams out of the casks.

"Mr Dale?" I ask, in a second of quiet.

"What is it?" he replies. He's older, wizened. Nut-like. His skin is permanently brown from the polishes and stains. His eyes, bright blue and keen, flicker across his work.

"You saw a murder – Lady Grey?"

"What of it?" he asks, still not looking my way.

"What did you see? Who did you see?"

Finally he lifts his greasy leather hat and looks up at me. "You're that kid from the theatre."

"I am — and it's Walter from the theatre that's been arrested."

He lays down the hammer and wipes sweat from his face with the filthiest cloth I've ever seen.

"Walter, eh? That the fellow who always plays the hero?"

I nod. "Yes."

"Short one? Stocky legs — like table legs."

I think about Walter's legs. "Yes. I suppose they are a little like a table."

"Not 'im." Mr Dale picks up his hammer and slams down on a nail.

"Sorry?"

"Not 'im, I say." Mr Dale bashes the nail again. "The person I saw, hopping off from the bloodbath — which I may say, I didn't actually see — it wasn't 'im. Person I saw was far taller, with elegant legs. Not table legs. I was on the other side of the river, mind."

I feel as if the sun's come out in this dark hole. "Would you swear to that?"

"Court of law, I would."

"Thank you, thank you, Mr Dale."

"Not that I want to see your Walter back on the

stage – terrible actor."

"He's not that bad," I say, feeling the smile cracking my face.

"Oh yes he is. Awful bad." But Mr Dale looks up at me with a grin. "But I'll tell you something for nothing. Whoever it was running away – they were wearing a dark-red cape. Crimson. Wool, I'd say."

"Well, Walter wasn't."

He nods. "Off you go then. Tell him I'd stand as his witness."

I step out of the door and then turn back in.

"Mr Dale, would you write that down? Sign it? It might make a difference."

"Hang on a mo." He stands and, still bent to the shape of his stool and his bench, shuffles to the side. He peels a printed ballad from the wall and turns it over. Lumps of flour glue shatter as he brushes the back. Then, as slowly as I've ever seen a person move, he pens a long exact account in beautiful curling handwriting and signs it at the bottom.

"Rupert ... Ignatius ... Dale. There," he says, handing it to me. "Will that do you?"

"Yes, thank you, yes!"

Punching the air, I run away from the boot shop, my heart full of hope. Suddenly the whole wharf looks wonderful. Everything is marvellous. Perfect.

Easy. Just a few words from a man who knows.

I let out a tiny "Yip" and a passing sailor stares at me as if I'm crazed.

Chapter 17

When I get back I find Valentina caking her face in mud. Her little caged bird is on the table, flapping from perch to floor and back again.

"How do I look, Mouse?" she says, blowing me a kiss.

"You look perfect," I say without thinking. "But, Valentina, I've been to see a witness — Mr Dale at the bootmaker's — and he says it can't possibly be Walter that did the murder because he saw the person who did it and it wasn't Walter. And..." I pull the mangled ballad from my pocket and place it carefully in the corner of the mirror frame. "He wrote this. We've got proper proof that Walter can't have done it!"

"Did he, poppet?" she says, her hand wobbling as she traces black paste around her eyes so that it blobs into her eyelashes. She tuts, wiping it away, and pulls at the paper, leaving big muddy prints.

"Stop it," I say, grabbing the paper from her fingers. "You'll ruin it."

"Sorry," she says, picking the mud from her eye. "I just wondered what he'd said."

"He says he'll stand up in court."

"Does he?" she says, smearing the mud thicker across her forehead. "How did you find him?"

"I found those men, Jameson and Stuart, and I sat under the table in the inn listening to them."

"Oh, clever Mouse," she says. "Were you in disguise?"

"Of course," I say.

She looks at the paper, this time without touching it. "Nice handwriting," she says. "What did he see?"

"Not Walter – definitely not Walter. It's wonderful!"

Valentina puckers her lips and blows herself a kiss in the mirror, then turns her gaze on me. "Sweetie, are you really trying to get Walter freed on your own? It's awfully dangerous. I mean, if Walter didn't do it, then there's a real murderer out there somewhere. If you're poking about—"

"No one will notice me. I'm always in disguise. So now we can help Walter. It might be that this piece of paper is enough. We may not need your captain – although perhaps he's got the connections to get Walter freed. Maybe he'd know who to give the piece of paper to. If I give it to Jameson and Stuart, they might ignore it because it doesn't fit their case." I stop. So many thoughts crowding for space. "Oh, and the real murderer had a dark-red cape. If we found out who owned that, it would definitely get Walter out."

Valentina wrinkles her nose and her face cracks. "D'you know, little one, I think now –" she draws a muddy line on my forehead – "when I've washed my face, would be a good time for us to visit Walter. You can bring him more food and tell him your good news yourself. We'll put you in a dress for the occasion. It pays to look powerful when you visit a prison."

"You'll come with me?"

"Of course, Mouseling." She pulls me close so that the mud from her face peels off on to my shirt. "Walter is my friend too."

"Oh, thank you, Valentina!" I lean forward to kiss her and she pushes me away.

"I'll get some candles, little rabbit. He'll need those. And you run up to his bed and find him a clean shirt. He must still be covered in blood."

Chapter 18

My heart floating above my head, the sky bright and full of birdsong, I run up the other set of stairs that lead from the stage. At the very top is Walter's tiny room, a bed and some shelves rammed up against the rafters with the smallest window above. All around the window are playbills and dried flowers, each pinned on top of the other, dating back to Walter's first performance long before I arrived. I take a moment to sit on his bed and gaze up at the curling undersides of the playbills. Sometimes Adam and I would hide up here when we were little and avoiding Eve. We made dens in Walter's bed.

I bury my face in Walter's pillow, the smell musky, comforting. When I was five I had a fever and slept here. I was burning up, and in my dreams I thought my legs would catch fire they were so hot. Walter had to look after me for days. He must have slept on the floor. I wonder how he did that, as well as act.

Taking a last sniff of comfort I shake the pictures out of my head and find him two clean shirts and some trousers. I pull the bedcover straight, sweep a cobweb from the window and pick my way back down the stairs. Maybe I'll try and get his sheets changed for when he comes home.

Dog and Kwadwo are waiting at the bottom. Valentina must have told Kwadwo we were going.

"No, Dog, you can't come. You stay here," I tell him.

Dog settles at Kwadwo's feet as Kwadwo lays a cloth over a fruited cake in the bottom of a basket. "Give him my love," he says, handing it over.

Five minutes later, dressed in our finest flowery gowns, we're skipping away from the theatre, our skirts held up over our knees to avoid the mud. Like a queen, Valentina sweeps through the streets, the embroidered flowers on the muslin heavy enough to softly bump into passers-by. I notice how people stare as we approach, as if she really is some kind of royalty. I stand taller, my neck straight, and I try to look ahead, not down, pretending to be so confident that there's no way I can trip or fall into something disgusting in the gutter. But I've grown in recent months and my dress is too tight. I can't raise my arms without the seams groaning and I'm already sweating, the handle of the basket slippery in my hand.

Running to catch up with her, I ask, "Will we go straight back after seeing Walter?"

"I wondered if we couldn't meet someone, poppet. What do you think?"

"Who?"

"Captain Teach."

"That would be wonderful. Now we have a witness, he can help us get Walter out of prison. Do you think he will?"

But she doesn't answer my question. Instead, she hooks the laces on my dress with one finger, pulling it tighter, and murmurs, "You know I told you about the queen last night. Remember, it's our secret. No telling Walter. No telling anyone."

"Why?"

She widens her silver-grey eyes. "Tempting fate," she says, before striding ahead. "We don't want everyone to know and then look foolish if it doesn't happen."

I'm thinking this through when she stops at a baker's and buys two loaves of bread. Passing a vegetable stall she buys a pomegranate and at the dairy, a lump of cheese. "That'll keep him going," she says, throwing it all in the basket with Kwadwo's cake and the shirts.

"When will you tell Mr Hawkin about the queen? We'll have to get the theatre ready. There's so much work to be done."

She puts a finger on my lip. "Shh, Mouse. All in good time. You'll make me wish I hadn't told you."

We approach the grubby lanes that surround the prison. Valentina's colours glow against the black stone. Flower-bright, she marches up to the front gate and pulls the bell. It sounds inside and brings on random rattles of chains and windows and bolts.

"Hark at that!" shouts one of the voices I heard last night. "A person at our drawbridge. Where's the servant to open it?"

Raucous laughter spills over the street and I step closer to Valentina.

A man eventually opens the door. He comes with the scent of fried bacon and old cabbage, and he peers at us from a bristle of greying hair that surrounds his whole face so that there is no border between his hair and his beard.

"We've come to see Walter. Walter Stroud," says Valentina. She's doing the full duchess thing, throwing her voice so that it rings around the street, bell-sharp and loud.

"And who might you be?" says the gaoler. He's pulling up his trousers as he begins to speak but by the time he's finished the sentence they're hanging down under his belly again.

"A friend." Valentina whispers the word and drops a coin into the gaoler's hand.

He stares at the silver coin bright against his earthy palm. "It's a very small coin," he says eventually.

I glance up at Valentina. The faintest look of panic crosses her face. I've almost never seen it before and then, as soon as it's there, it's gone.

"Here then." She drops a second, slightly larger, coin into his outstretched hand.

"Of course." He steps back, admitting us to a dark, rustling passage. "Enter, ladies."

Somebody somewhere giggles. It's not a friendly sound.

"A private audience?" Valentina suggests as we stand far too close to the bristly gaoler, unseen things squeaking around our feet.

The man holds his hand out again. I can't see her face but I can hear her irritation. She drops another small coin into his hand.

"This way," he says, leading us towards an even darker, narrower entrance that turns out to be a spiral staircase. I follow Valentina. Now we're away from the door, new smells fill every scrap of air. They're hideous. Every kind of smell: human, animal, dead, alive.

It's dark in this stairwell, and voices ring from the damp walls. Ahead of me, Valentina's dress billows out and she scoops it away from the stone. I clutch mine around my thighs. Things crunch and squish wetly under my boots. They could be snails or lemons; I wouldn't know.

We turn three times around the spiral and arrive at a tiny dark landing. Only the gaoler's lantern throws any light. There are no windows, and no air.

"This one," he says, unlocking a padlock and rattling a chain.

The smell that wafts out on the human heat is eye-watering.

"Whoa!" Valentina steps back, bumping into me, and I grab her arm. Under cover of her sleeve, we hold hands.

I suppose I'd expected Walter to have a room on his own, even a horrible dark, unlit room, but this is a cell crammed with people. They surge forwards.

"Stay back!" shouts the gaoler, and he waves a short heavy stick in the air. "These fine ladies are after Walter Stroud!"

"Here! Here I am," shouts Walter, and I can hear his voice clearly despite all the other occupants joining in.

"This grand person here wants to talk to you – so I will show you to a suite of suitable rooms," says the gaoler.

"The pit?" someone shouts.

"The long drop?" shouts another.

I back away, bumping against the slimy walls. Walter steps forward and the gaoler locks the door behind him.

"Valentina! Mouse!" Walter raises his arms to wave, which is when I see the shackle joining his hands together.

"This way, Romeo," interrupts the gaoler. "Down to the tennis court. You can have an intimate little chat there, just you, me and the ladies."

"No," says Valentina. "You will not be there, sir. We will see Walter on his own. It is his right."

"Oooooh!" says the gaoler. "Very demanding, aren't we? He's got no rights in here so that'll cost you, pretty lady."

Valentina's mouth is pinched as she hands over another coin.

We squeeze down the staircase, each on top of the other, and the gaoler opens a door into a small courtyard. There's a pump, a pool of fetid water beneath a heap of rubbish, and two cats playing with a squirrel's tail.

"Welcome to the tennis court. I'll give you till the clock strikes." He does a mock bow and disappears through a door.

Chapter 19

For a second we all stare at his retreating back.

"Thank you, thank you!" says Walter, throwing his shackled arms over my head and grasping me tight, giving me the closest of hugs. I press my face into his chest. He smells awful but underneath it he still smells of Walter. Words rumble in his chest and I'm barely listening, just feeling him and feeling so much better for being with him.

It's been barely any time but I've missed him so much. I look up through the funny fuzzy beard that's growing on his chin. His face is grey. Yellow-grey.

"Thank you for coming. I was beginning to feel as

if I'd been forgotten by everyone." There's a sob in his voice.

"Walter, Walter," says Valentina, using her stage voice. "We could never forget you – you're very important to us. I—"

"I've found a witness," I interrupt.

"What? Really? Who?"

"Tell us what *you* saw," Valentina cuts in. "We never had a chance to hear your side of the story because those vile men appeared."

"I told Mouse before – almost nothing," he says, looking up at the blue square of sky above us. "I remember walking through Queen Square. I was practising my lines and then there was a scream – a really terrified scream – so I ran towards it."

"Anything else?" asks Valentina. "Did you see anyone – perhaps anyone running away? Leaning over her? Carrying a weapon? Think! Mouse seems to think she can get you out of here. And that might depend on what you can remember." She pulls my head back from Walter's chest and holds it against hers.

"I don't know! Perhaps..." Still clutching my hand, Walter paces the tiny yard, catching the toe of his shoe under a corner of the rubbish heap. A shrew leaps out and the two cats spring. The shrew doesn't stand a chance. Valentina watches, open-mouthed, as the cats tear the tiny creature apart.

"What was it, Walter? You might have seen the same thing as the witness," I say.

"I think I saw a man – running. Nowhere near the woman but running away – running from the river." He looks up, squints. "A man with a cloak? Or a loose jacket? More of a shadow, perhaps, than a person – and it struck me at the time that they were running away from the scream, when they ought to have been running towards it, like I had. But I couldn't possibly identify them."

"A man in a cloak," I say. "That's what Mr Dale said. He's the witness. He came forward to Jameson and Stuart, the men who arrested you. He said you had legs like a table and the man he saw running away was more elegant."

"A table?" Walter laughs and looks down at his legs. "I suppose my calves are quite thick. But how did you find out there was a witness, Mouse? No one told me that."

"Mouse ..." Valentina flicks the end of my nose with her fingernail. It makes my eyes water, "... has used the skills she's been taught to the very best of her ability."

"I sneaked into their office – well, the White Lion – and listened in."

"You brave darling," says Walter, squeezing me close. He keeps sniffing. "So how is the theatre without me?"

"I'm having to play the leading man – and you know what that's like," says Valentina, watching the cats licking their paws.

Walter winces. "Sorry, Valentina. That's grim. The audience – are they being kind?"

Valentina grins. "Mrs H is the leading lady. She's having the toughest time." She runs a finger down his cheek. "But we need to get you out of here. We must find you a lawyer."

"Doesn't having a witness prove Walter didn't do it?"

Valentina shakes her head. "No, duckling, it doesn't. It has to be discussed in a court of law. Walter is here until we can prove he's innocent."

"But that's so unfair!" Rain clouds gather over my sunny mood. I hadn't expected this.

Walter nods. "Lawyers are expensive and I've only got a few coins – if Hawkin hasn't helped himself to them."

"But your man, Captain Teach," I say. "Valentina? He'll help, won't he?"

"Of course, poppet." A broad warm smile breaks over her face. "He's working on it as we speak.

Have heart, dear Walter," she says, squeezing his chin. "Have heart."

We leave, giving Walter the contents of the basket. He's especially excited by the clean shirts.

The gaoler reappears and shoos us out, waving goodbye and blowing a kiss.

"Loathsome man," says Valentina as we step out through the doorway. "Awful place."

I look back up at the side of the building. There at the very top is Walter's hand, waving. Pale against the blackened sooty stone. "Thank you!" he calls, and the whole building breaks into a peal of mocking imitations.

Valentina's skirt billows as she stomps away from the prison. She walks so fast, I'm almost running by the time we pass the castle and suddenly we break into the fresh air near the market.

"Oh!" She stops and flaps at her face with her handkerchief. "So glad to get away from that place. Simply vile."

"Poor things," I say. "I wonder what most of them have done to deserve it."

Valentina glances sideways at me. "You're too nice, Mouse."

"Well, I do. I mean, you can be locked up for

stealing some bread — but suppose you're starving?"

"Stop there," she says, pulling me into a shady doorway. She produces a brush from the little bag that hangs from her belt and drags it roughly through my knotty hair. "Those people let themselves get caught. Let themselves go. Just dreadful!" She brushes harder.

"Ow!" I say. "You're hurting me."

"Captain Teach can't see you like this. We must get that prison out of your hair."

"Have you told him about the queen coming? I didn't tell Walter, even though I wanted to. And do you really trust Captain Teach? He looks like a pirate!"

"Shhh. Too many questions." She sweeps the brush right across the back of my hair.

"Ow!" I say as she drags out a huge knot. I push her away. She's being weird. I want her to concentrate on Walter but I'm sensing that she's got her own agenda and I don't know what it is.

She pulls make-up from her bag, puffs powder on my face and draws with a purple stick on my lips.

"No matter how smart I look it's not going to make any difference to Walter, is it?" I ask.

Valentina widens her eyes and looks into a tiny mirror. "Appearance always matters. You should always be dressed for the part." She fastens a small green-glass necklace around my neck. "If you're playing the urchin then rub dirt in your face, scrape the ground. If a queen, you must have velvet and gold and stand like a goddess. There are times to be invisible and times to be seen. And we want to be taken seriously. Got it? Anyway. That'll do," she says. "Curtsy for me. Let's take a look at you."

She hands me the mirror. Instead of me I see a girl with almost straight black hair, brown eyes and soft brown skin. She has a strange purple mouth and when I smile I see her lips move too.

"Different," I whisper.

"Yes," Valentina breathes into my ear. "Different. That's the art, Mouse, being different. Be different every time and no one will ever quite know who you really are."

Chapter 20

Valentina pops the mirror back in her bag and marches off, leaving me standing in the alley. I run to catch up, copying her long strides. I'm not so good at this. Also, it's hot in this dress, and the skirts catch on things so it's awkward to walk. I try to do the head-in-the-air thing, looking down my nose, but my make-up's running and I'm sweating. I am not looking queenly. The sweat has already made the back of my dress wet and I can feel it trickling down behind my knees.

"How do you know he'll be here?" I whisper.

"He's always here. Never leaves his ship."

"Valentina!" I hiss. "My make-up's all over my face."

She swings to look at me.

"It isn't, you're fine. Be brave, dollkin."

We glide towards Narrow Quay. Or at least, Valentina glides.

I can barely keep up with her. We get down on to the quay where the men are loading and unloading the ships. The sailors stare as she cuts through them, smiling and laughing and looking so fine.

"Valentina!"

Ignoring me, she dives into the muddle of sailors and traders that line the quays and, given no choice, I follow.

I've nothing to steal but I hoist my skirts well above my knees and hold tight to them. By now my purple lip colour must be all over my face but all I can do is try and keep up and, after the gloomy news that having a witness doesn't let a person off, visiting Captain Teach gives the faintest uplift to my heart.

I want to ask Valentina more questions, but she's going so fast, I can't get alongside her until suddenly she pauses at *The Running Stag*.

She points to a shady wall some distance away. "Stay there," she whispers, and then marches up to the ship. "Captain Teach?" she demands of the air.

"And who wants him?" shouts a man from the top of the mast.

I lurk in the shade watching Valentina being a duchess, but also watching everyone moving around us. I've spent my whole life in the theatre and we have every sort of person, but here on the quay the cutthroats and pickpockets are half the population and in this stupid dress I'm an absolute target.

"'Scuse me," scrapes a voice too close for comfort. I turn, so close I can smell him, to a ragged man. He fixes me with his single eye.

"What you doing here, squib?" he says. "On your own, eh?"

"No," I say, refusing to look at him. "I'm with her — with that ship." I point at *The Running Stag*.

"Oh!" he says, and melts away.

I glance back at the ship. Valentina's still waiting, and whether because of her or because of the crew, passers-by seem to give the ship a wide berth. No one wants to come too close. While I'm watching, the tall man with the black beard races down a ladder and they have a whispered conversation. Valentina waves her arms about and says something that makes him raise his eyebrows then laugh. It finishes with them doing an Italian kiss, like Mr Hawkin makes the lovers do when we're doing the comedy plays. I can't hear any of it because the sounds of clanking and banging that surround the harbour make listening impossible.

They touch hands and then she turns to look for me. She's smiling as she dances over the ropes and clutter of the quayside.

"Good?" I ask.

"All good," she replies, and races off ahead of me, sweeping a way through the crowds on the quay, turning right over the bridge and charging on towards the theatre. "Captain Teach will definitely help me with a little problem."

"Help you?" I say.

But she skips away towards the theatre and with not the faintest trace of grace, I follow.

Chapter 21

When we get back, the first thing I notice is that the theatre stinks. But when we run upstairs to look for the source of the smell, I find my statement from Mr Dale has vanished.

"Where is it? It was here, by the mirror. Where's it gone, Valentina?"

She looks behind the mirror and under the table. "I don't know, Mouse. You must have put it somewhere safe. It can't be far away."

"I didn't put it anywhere. I left it here."

"Perhaps you put it somewhere else," she says, sticking a crust of bread through the bars of the bird's cage and examining her face in the mirror.

"No, I didn't," I mutter.

I look everywhere. There's no sign of it ever having existed.

I ask everyone else. Mr Hawkin stares at me as if I'm mad. "The smell, child, the smell – much more important."

Kwadwo says he'll keep an eye out. Bridget's searching the corners of the costume store for the source of the smell and says she hasn't seen it.

As I search for the letter, I join the search for the smell. At first it comes and goes, one minute there, the next vanished. It's at its worst at the top of the stairs, but then it fades for a while. I search the cupboards in the costume room, the space under the stage, and all the way up to the heavenly balcony at the top.

"I smell a rat," says Eve. "It's little Mouse; she's gone off."

"Have you seen a letter? A scroll, written on a ballad?"

She shakes her head. A flicker in her eyes tells me that she didn't know about it. That counts her out.

But I think she's right about the smell. It *is* a rat and it'll only get worse.

While Valentina puts fresh make-up on for this

evening, I empty the hampers. I take out all the dresses and cloaks and shake them. Apparently, Bridget did it earlier but the stink feels like it comes from somewhere really close. And perhaps my piece of paper got in there too.

Mr Hawkin stamps past holding some lemon peel under his nose, like that's going to make any difference.

"Any luck, lambkin?" asks Valentina. "No rat, no letter?"

"No." I wrench the top from the large hamper that Walter hid in and pull out an assortment of coats and blankets. Most of them are natural colours, browns and beiges, but at the bottom, crumpled into a corner, is a dark-red wool blanket.

Red? Isn't that the colour Mr Dale said he saw?

I unfold it across the bottom of the basket. It would be a full-length cloak on me, but on a taller person, a cape. Very slowly, and with my arms still hanging over the side of the hamper, I check it. There's a blob of darker red on it, brown really, and it's thick and heavy. Maybe it's oxblood – the stuff we use in the theatre. Or maybe it isn't.

I've never seen this garment before.

I glance around. Eve is stitching feathers, Bridget mending shoes, Kwadwo has a lantern in his hands. Behind me Valentina is pinning her hair up under a wig, concentrating. Mr Hawkin appears at the top of the stairs, closely followed by Ambrose, who stops and stares at the blankets lying on the ground.

I throw the cloaks and capes back in the basket and slam the lid closed.

What have I just found?

"Company! Company!" Mr Hawkin is still clutching his lemon peel. "We've got an audience; time to give them a show. Now, this dire smell has leaked out into the auditorium but I do believe that the unwashed nature of our patrons will mask it. After the performance we can take the whole building apart if necessary."

"Wings!" demands Eve, and automatically I scurry around to sort out her harness. She stands with her back to me and her arms out. "Still not found your dead relative, Mouse?"

I decide not to answer. The rat smell is nothing compared to the blanket in the hamper. It was a red blanket, exactly as Mr Dale described.

"Pity. I suspect it's close to home. Your home." She turns and looks at me, her face brushing the wing. A picture of innocence.

"You — you know where it is?"

But all she does is smile.

With my head thinking about the red blanket, my hands search my bed. The smell *is* very strong, but there are no dead things on my shelf or anywhere I can find. My stomach full of dread, I go back down and lace myself into my dress for the performance.

The play's hard work. Wafts of rat billow over the stage from time to time and the audience notice and all the time I'm thinking about who hid the blanket. Whoever put it there probably stole Mr Dale's statement.

And they're probably the murderer.

"Keep going! Keep going!" shouts Mr Hawkin, racing offstage and rummaging in the props cupboard for an incense burner.

Which means the murderer is in the theatre.

Is one of us.

Valentina, dressed as Walter, carries the incense burner using it as a lantern, puffing the smoke across the audience.

It smells worse.

We stagger through to the end of the play. I want to take another look at that blanket but I can't do it while everyone's still searching for the rat. And somehow I don't think the stink reached its deadly hiding place all on its own.

As I'm searching our massive collection of mangled

shoes, Ambrose sweeps past. "Did I hear you found a witness?"

"Yes," I say slowly. "Yes, and he signed a statement."

"Ah – the one you've lost. Who is he?"

"Mr Dale, at the boot shop. I'm going to go back and see him first thing. Get another statement."

"I know him. What did he say?"

"He saw an elegant man running from the quayside. It wasn't Walter. Definitely not Walter."

Ambrose raises an eyebrow. "Good work, Mouse." He checks his reflection in a shard of mirror. "Still no sign of that rat, eh?"

I watch him pull a hair from his nostril and wince. Could it be him?

"Mouse! Mouse!" calls Eve. She's standing with her wings and her arms spread right next to Valentina, waiting for my help. I'd like to leave her there, but this is my job. Eve turns around so that she's facing Valentina, but I'm glad to see Valentina ignores her. She's too busy tucking her hair under a knitted cap.

I begin to unbuckle the harness. In an extra-loud voice, Eve says, "Oh, and when you've finished that, I left my halo on the stage. Rescue it, would you, Mouseling?"

The last buckle comes undone and I run down from the costume store to the stage. It's dark down here now so I have to kick my way across the boards in the hope of finding the stupid halo. Eventually I come across it at the back of the stage. It could have stayed there until the morning. With the plummeting feeling that I've been sent on a wild goose chase, I pick it up and race up to the costume store, but I'm too late. I can hear the fuss coming from my quarters right up in the roof.

"Here!" shouts Bridget. "I've found the rat, but look – look at this!"

"What? What is it?" Eve's voice. "Where? Oh! How horrid!"

"The rat?" calls Mr Hawkin. "You've found the critter?"

All the calls are coming from my eyrie. I knew it. I just knew it.

"They're up in your space, Mouse," says Adam.

"I know!" I say.

"Eve's found it."

"That's because she put it there," I mutter.

"Care to say that louder, so that everyone can hear?" says Eve, clambering across the hampers. "And care to explain that picture you carved in the wood?"

"What picture?" asks Adam.

"There are some pictures she's carved!" Eve sobs. "All of us, our whole theatre family, nasty caricatures.

And the one of me! It's horrid! Cruel and ugly."

I look around for Valentina's help, but she's not here.

"Mouse?" says Bridget, stumbling from the hampers, swinging the rat by his tail. "What's the meaning of those horns?"

"I was angry," I say. "Eve had—"

"Ma, she's being cruel." Eve turns towards her mother, who looks bewildered, glances at me, stares at Eve and then says, "All cats are grey in the dark."

"What's going on?" asks Mr Hawkin.

Bridget opens a window and flings the rat out into the night. "We followed the smell – or rather, Eve followed the smell up to Mouse's little pad. And we found the rat."

"Where was it?" asks Adam.

"Up on the beam. Must have just died there," says Eve, breaking off from her theatrical sobbing.

"Clever girl for spotting it," says Bridget. "I could smell it, but I couldn't see it anywhere. And such a funny place to die."

"Wasn't it?" I mutter.

The whole Hawkin family and Bridget cram up on to the hampers, attempting to look at the same time.

Ambrose strolls through from the back of the theatre where he's been drinking with some of the audience. "Have they found the rat?"

I nod.

He looks up. "In your bed?" he asks.

"More or less."

"Do you think it got itself there?"

I shake my head.

"She's a nasty piece of work. Mind your back," he says, wiping red wine from his lips on a cloth. "Night then. See you tomorrow."

I think of the red cloak. And as I watch him leave I notice how long and elegant his legs are.

Chapter 22

The costume store stays the centre of attention and I get no chance to pull the blanket out of the hamper. All of it makes me late taking food for Walter. I keep my dress on and jam a jacket over the top. There's no way I'm going up to my space to change. As I leave, I try hard not to listen to the things that Eve's saying, but I can't help hearing them.

"She's mean and horrible and we should cast her out."

I hear a rumbling reply from her father.

"But that drawing is nasty and vicious, and she needs to be punished." I'd swear Eve's projecting her voice on purpose so that it reaches me.

"Cruel is as cruel does," mutters her mother.

"What does that mean, woman?" demands Mr Hawkin.

I don't bother to find out.

It's still warm and my boots seem unnecessarily hot but I don't want to walk through the scuttling mud without proper covering. "Here, Dog," I say. He rises slowly from his haunches. He's getting stiffer and, not for the first time, I wonder how long dogs live for.

Downstairs, Kwadwo's waiting with the basket of food for Walter. "Go carefully."

"I will," I say, pocketing a handful of pebbles from the ground just in case my tune doesn't summon Walter. I'm about to leave the theatre when a voice calls me from behind. It's Adam. He's standing on a step, but I notice for the first time that he's taller than me.

From here, he looks older.

"She did it. You know that though," he says.

"I do," I say. "Why didn't you stop her?"

"Don't know," he says. I sense that he's looking away from me now, probably at the floor.

"I'll stop her next time," he sniffs.

"Really?" I ask.

"Can I stroke Dog?" he whispers.

I pause. Remembering him warm and soft and sharing my pillow, his tiny hand in mine when he was little. "Yes," I say in the end. "You can stroke Dog."

Dog and I lope over the mud and out into the town. I'm regretting the dress. The chunky hem catches under my feet and I run too slowly to feel safe. I should have changed. And I should have taken that blanket out of the hamper before it disappears too. I'll have to do it when I get back. The warehouses loom out of the dark, creatures skulking around the bottoms of the walls. I reach the main quay where the masts are silhouetted against the sky. Here, hundreds of cables clank softly as the boats bob on the tide, and there are lanterns burning on some of them. A few figures stumble around alongside the ships and I keep well clear, lurking with the rats until I reach the bridge.

I pause there to avoid a small group of noisy sailors making their way along the far bank. They'd probably ignore me but I don't want to have to find out. After throwing punches at each other they stumble off in different directions and I take my chance to scuttle over the bridge, staying low, keeping below the parapet.

As I descend the cobbles on the far side, I glance to my left along towards Welsh Back. Standing by a lantern is the lanky figure of Captain Teach. He's talking to a tall slender man. But there's something about the way the other man's standing – and with a jolt, I realise it's Valentina in costume. I stop, watching them between the balustrades. They're whispering, urgently, and then she hands him something that clanks.

Money? Why's she giving him money? I'd expect it to be the other way round.

Valentina finally leaves the captain and, breaking into a run, she swings round on to the bridge and heads towards the theatre, her boots skimming Dog's tail.

"All good?" Valentina asks on my return. She's sitting in front of the make-up mirror, dabbing cream around her eyes.

"Yes," I say. "I gave Walter his food. Did I see you out by the bridge?"

"No, poppet. You must be mistaken. I'd have loved to go out, it's been very dull here, hasn't it, birdy?" she says, holding up the birdcage and peering at me through the bars.

I loiter, undressing near the hampers for as long as I dare, but she's taking an age to remove her make-up. I'm not going to be able to get the blanket out now.

Instead I take a stub of candle, clamber up to my bed and lie there watching the light flickering over my carved figures.

With Dog's head heavy on my ankles I think about Valentina. About everything I've seen this evening.

Why did she lie?

"What do you think, Dog?" I whisper. But he's already asleep.

Chapter 23

When I wake the next morning, Dog's not there and, below me, Bridget's rustling around in the piles of shoes.

"Dog?" I call him. He doesn't appear and I begin to worry. He's old. Stiff. He could crawl off to die and I wouldn't know.

"Dog?" I shout, and run downstairs into the theatre just in time to see Mr Hawkin hand Dog's lead to Eve.

"What?" My voice bounces back from the galleries, releasing three seagulls and a pigeon into the fresh morning air.

Mr Hawkin turns, rolls his eyes and mutters something that might be "Sanctions" under his breath.

Eve smiles. It's not a nice smile.

I open my mouth to protest but Kwadwo appears alongside me and puts one finger to my lips. "Shhh, stop," he says. "He's given her Dog."

"What? I don't understand. Why?"

Kwadwo raises an eyebrow. "Why do you think?"

I feel suddenly sick. "To get back at me for the carvings? But she can't have him!"

"Shhh. Shh, Mouse. She can. She has." He puts his hand on mine. "He's Mr Hawkin's dog and she's Mr Hawkin's daughter. I don't think there's anything you can do."

The shock leaves me numb. And a few minutes later when Eve emerges again with Dog at her side, it feels as if it's happening to someone else.

"Sit, Dog. Sit!" she says. Dog glances up at her and lowers himself slowly to the ground. The moment he's down, she yanks his collar. "No, stand. Come on!" She tugs on the lead and with a bewildered look in his eye he follows her, his feet shuffling. As they walk up to the Hawkins' quarters, Dog glances back at me.

"I'm sorry," I whisper.

I'm angry, so angry I can barely walk straight.

How could they? How could Mrs Hawkin let Dog go to Eve? She knows what he means to me. And she's usually so kind. And Mr Hawkin. He's not an unreasonable man. He's normally fair and this is *so* unfair. And why didn't Kwadwo say something?

I stop at the top of the stairs and think, and I feel angrier. It's not just Dog, it's Valentina. What's she doing running around the harbour giving sea captains money? Why's she being even more secretive than usual? Why is she lying? I march up into the empty costume room, pull open the big hamper, burrow down to the bottom and yank the blanket out. I hide it in a cloth bag, storm out of the theatre and cross the bridge towards the boot-mender's shop.

At least I can get another statement from Mr Dale. And show him the blanket; ask him if it's the same one.

The door's open so I stick my head into the dark shop and wait for my eyes to adjust to the light. Where Mr Dale usually sits is a boy, surrounded by the muddle of several pairs of mismatched boots. He's bashing away on the anvil, like Mr Dale might if he was drunk, but not at all like a real bootmaker. The hammer bounces off a nail and flies out of his hand, smashing into the corner of the room.

"Aargh!" shouts the boy. "Stupid thing!"

I pick his hammer up from the floor and hand it back to him. "Hello," I say. "Where's Mr Dale?"

"Why?" he asks. "My boot-mending not good enough for you?"

"I'm not after boot-mending. I want a word with him if he's around?"

"Well, he isn't and I don't know where he is."

My stomach sinks. "Since when?"

"He didn't arrive this morning. I came in, and they keep asking for their boots, and I'm trying to keep up. I can't spend all day talking to you." His greasy hair flops over his face. "Pass us that pair over there."

I pick up a pair of black boots that look the same as all the others and hand it to him.

"So when did you last see him?"

The boy's hammer bounces three times from the boots in front of him – each time missing the nail head.

"Why? Who wants to know?"

"I do," I say.

He scowls at me. "I'm not even a boot-mender – I only get the leather and drop the boots back to the customers. I don't know how to do it."

I look down at his awful efforts. I can't think of anything nice to say.

"So have you any idea where he is?"

He looks at me mournfully. "No. I haven't seen him since work yesterday. He lives upstairs and he's not there either. Now, will you go away, please?"

Chapter 21

When I get back to the theatre, I want to challenge her, but Valentina is showing her wild side. There doesn't seem to be a reason, but she's bounding around the costume store crashing into things like a cockchafer. She is wearing a dress embroidered with green iridescent beetle wings and her hair is swept up so that it forms a radiant crown around her head. Today she's a freshly hatched insect trapped inside the walls of the theatre, her colours so vivid.

"Mr Dale seems to have disappeared. So's his statement," I say. "And Eve has stolen Dog."

Valentina pauses, crouched, ready to spring. She

frowns, and then a soft smile creases her cheeks. "Oh, Mouse, that's horrible!" She sweeps a silk scarf over my shoulders. "So – you need cheering up. Instead of fighting, why don't we dance for today's lesson? You like dancing, don't you? Change your shoes, lambkin. We'll use the auditorium."

Missing my Dog shadow, I change my boots for dancing shoes, hide the blanket safely under my bed and run down from the top to the bottom of the theatre.

"Music!" she shouts into the air as if there was a magical orchestra hidden under the stage. "Now, Mouse, stand tall and you lead."

I have dancing lessons from Valentina all the time, lots of them, alongside fencing, fighting, acting, gymnastics and singing and all the arts we have to be able to do in the theatre, but usually Walter or Ambrose will play a tune. I used to have them with Eve and Adam – but Valentina took over a couple of years ago and she pulled me away from the other two. "You, Mouse, are too good to learn alongside them. You are –" and she pulled my face to hers – "a *talent*."

I've never quite understood what she meant, but I am better at fighting and gymnastics, and probably acting. I'm not sure it makes me a talent but doubt that Eve's much good at anything except floating over the stage with her wings on. And Adam's only little.

As well as the lack of music, there's something different today. Valentina is wilder. Her steps are huge, and the imaginary tune playing in her head takes us in vast looping circles around the stage and even out through the doors.

She sweeps me along, her leading, then me leading, cutting our way over the mud and back into the theatre. "Good work, Mouse. You're doing well. To be the leading actor in this shabby ship you must learn to lead, and learn to follow. Now – faster!" She beats out a rhythm with her heel and we gallop across the floor, side to side, back and forth. Straw rises from the ground and the whirling air settles dust on my sweating face. Kwadwo sticks his head out from his dark corridor and laughs at us. He disappears and comes back with a flat drum that he beats with a short stick.

He plays the rhythm, increasing the pace, and Valentina and I fall over each other to speed up, tumbling and leaping and holding each other up and her dress bounces around us and her hair falls out of its pins and the dance becomes like a fight, faster and faster and I can't let go, but I can't breathe, and my feet barely touch the ground. We blunder into the side of the stage and back to the centre of the floor.

Crash.

My hip hits the corner of a table, but Valentina won't let me go; we're bound together. Stumbling, tripping, whirling – crashing into the gallery, the balustrades, the stage again.

"Stop!" I shout. "I can't—"

"Yes, you can!" shouts Valentina, her eyes wide, her mouth wider. Her hair's all over her face, strands caught in her mouth and stuck to her skin. Her red lips have slid across her face. She looks mad.

Dog runs down from the balcony and barks at the side. Leaping and snapping at Valentina's spinning skirts.

Eve appears beside him, and stops, open-mouthed, gazing at Valentina as she whoops and swoops.

And then there are three of us dancing. Not Eve, but Kwadwo. He drops the drum and grabs my arm, pulling me from Valentina. He whisks her away and I watch them whirl and stamp and leap together while I get my breath back.

I stagger to stop the world spinning, and focus on Eve. Her face crumples, as if she's going to cry. She sticks her tongue out at me and turns for the stairs, dragging Dog behind her. He lingers at the bottom and gives me a long, soulful look.

I'm staring at the empty Dog space when Valentina

charges past again and sucks me forwards, and then again the three of us are dancing and I just about manage to stay upright when Kwadwo trips and pulls us all down and we fall in a heap in a patch of dusty sunlight.

Valentina collapses back and lies flat on the straw, Kwadwo leaps to his feet and when I look round he's gone. "You're really quite good," says Valentina quietly. "You'll be dispensing with me soon, little dove."

"No, Valentina," I say. "I can't dance like you, or fight, or act."

She rolls over and fixes her cool eyes on mine. "Won't be long before you're good enough to perform for a queen. You're nearly there, poppet. You're nearly there."

"Is it definite? Can we tell everyone?" I whisper.

Valentina taps the side of her nose. "Shhh," she says. "Almost. Almost."

Chapter 25

The moment we've finished, I run up to take another look at the blanket. It's got no moth holes, which means it's not been in the building long, because the moths attack all the wool in this place.

And the patch of blood is thick – not like our fake blood. Although perhaps Walter got the blood on it when he hid? But the blanket wasn't there when he hid. I saw the bottom of the hamper.

It really wasn't.

Which means someone put it there afterwards. I've a horrible feeling I know who.

I'll pick up today's posters from the printer's, and

I'll go and see Mr Dale again, show it to him.

I run straight to Mr Dale's workshop but the shop's all shut up, no sign even of the boy from this morning. Standing on a box I peer through a murky pane of glass into the unlit interior. It's all dark and there's definitely no one in there. The windows are shut upstairs.

I walk to the end of the row and turn left as if I was going to the printing shop. I swing around the corner and I notice a gated snicket running along the back of the buildings, linking all their yards. I look around to see if anyone would notice if I took a look, but they're all too busy getting drunk and into fights. I open the gate, stepping smartly into the first yard; it's mostly heaped with rubbish. The next has vegetables growing and is neater so I run on through in case I'm spotted. "Six, seven, eight." I stop. This must be the one. There are six tall barrels lined up behind, and the yard gives on to the brewery at the back.

Shuffling a fruit box closer to a small window, I step on it and try to see through the glass. It's too high so I grab the nearest barrel and use the top of it to haul myself higher, so that I have one foot on the side of the barrel and one on the wall.

There's a weird smell. Not only beer. Sweeter.

Pressing my nose to the glass I peer through, but

the window's filthy. I try wiping it with my cuff but I still can't see a thing. Above me the glass looks cleaner; perhaps I could get up there.

Gripping the top of the barrel with both hands, I hoist myself higher and get a better look into the workshop, but really there's nothing to see that I haven't already seen.

Off to my left someone gets going with a saw and a babble of voices rise from children on the other side of the wall. I should get down.

I glance down to make sure that my feet land in the right place and catch a glimpse of something in the barrel. I have to stare at it for a full minute before I realise that I'm looking at Mr Dale.

And he's definitely dead.

Chapter 26

Running and vomiting isn't easy, but fear gives a person superhuman powers. I race away from the buildings back on to the quayside. Everyone's behaving normally, talking to each other and shouting and fighting and I want to shout at them, "I've found a body. I've found a body!"

I bite down a last wave of vomit and look at all the ships. There must be a person in charge. A harbourmaster? But all I see are stumbling pirates and broken sailors, busy merchants and downtrodden women. None of them look any use at all when I think back to the thing I've just seen. I shudder.

And then I see the two men who arrested Walter. Jameson and Stuart. The Queen's Officers. They're walking among the ships, asking questions.

I wonder if they'd believe me.

I wonder if they'll recognise me? That would be trouble.

I take off my jacket and tie it around my waist, so that it hangs skirt-wise. My shirt is baggy, so I roll up the sleeves to the elbow so that it looks smaller. I take off my boots and leave them with the blanket under a pile of ropes, rubbing my feet into the dirt so they turn grey. I brush my hair down into a plait so that it hangs more like a pirate's than a girl's. Picking up some charcoal from the ground, I crumble it to rub around my eyes and up and down my arms. I'm now filthy, and worn, and much more of an urchin than a child from the theatre. At least, I hope I am.

While I'm getting ready, I practise an accent. I've heard people from up the country and I can do the sounds. "Here – there, what I saw. I saw – summat 'orrible." I keep muttering to myself as I wander over to the men. I need more urgency in my step. I need to look like I just ran from the place.

"Sir – sir!" I shout. Doing my best northern voice.

They completely ignore me.

"'Scuse me! I need some 'elp!"

The younger one turns his head and looks across to me. A squint of recognition crosses his face to be replaced by a blank look of confusion. He points to himself as if I might be shouting at someone else.

"Yes, you!" I shout, suddenly realising that if I'd never met them before I wouldn't know they were anything to do with the law. But it's too late now. He tilts his head and I pick my way through the ropes on the quay. "I've found summat nasty behind yon cottages," I say. Keeping the accent is like walking a tightrope. If I say too much, too fast, I'll fall off the side and they'll know. "Over yon." I point towards the boot-mender's shop.

"What, tiddler?" he says, tapping his friend on the shoulder.

"Somebody's in a barrel. Smell as offal." Will he understand me?

"Offal?" says the older one.

"Bad," I say in explanation. "Dead. Over yon."

His eyes follow the direction of my finger. I don't want to stay here any longer than I have to but he's not getting it. "I'll show ya," I say, walking away towards the boot-mender's shop.

The tall one follows me and the short one stands staring at me but doesn't move.

I don't want to get too close; it might remind them

that they've seen me before. Instead I walk backwards, beckoning, moving every part of my body in a way that isn't me so that they don't get the similarity.

"All right, all right, I'm coming."

"S'round t'back," I say, skipping towards the entrance to the snicket. "You wanna go right down by t'brewery. 'E's in t'biggest barrel, right next to 'ouse."

Curiosity piqued, Stuart brushes past me and makes his way down the alley until he reaches the right yard. I should run at this point, get out of the way, but I want to be sure he sees it.

I'm stupid because Jameson appears behind me and waits.

"Go on!" he shouts. "What is it? What can you see?"

"There's a rope, a ship's rope, tarry, going into this 'ere barrel," says Stuart, picking up the end of a rope from the ground.

"Tha'rt should join 'im," I say, standing back and pointing.

Jameson glares at me, but he sets off down the alley and is halfway down when the first one finds Mr Dale.

"Oh, lord!" he says. "Oh—" And he vomits right next to where I did.

I'm gone before they come back. Grabbing my bag

and boots, I run barefoot to the printer's and hang around behind his shop, hoping to forget what I saw.

Poor Mr Dale.

That wasn't an accident. Whoever killed Lady Grey must have done it.

It dashes Walter's hopes of clearing his name. There were no other witnesses and I've lost Mr Dale's statement.

This is terrible.

The printer hands me a bundle of posters and I stare at them in my hands.

I don't think I can put these up everywhere. I don't think I feel strong enough to do it.

Poor Mr Dale.

Chapter 27

I get back minutes before the performance and run to stuff the red blanket under my bed. As I head to the stage I find Valentina in the wings twisting paper into spills for lighting candles. I wasn't going to tell her about Mr Dale but when I see her I can't help myself. "Mr Dale's dead," I say.

"Who, poppet?"

"The witness."

She swings round, her mouth dropping open. "How do you know that?"

"I saw him. Dead."

Valentina puts her hand to her mouth, her eyes

opening wide. "Oh, Mouse, you didn't! Where?"

"In a barrel."

"That's dreadful!"

"It is! He was the only witness that's come forward."

She shakes her head. "No, no. I'm shocked that you saw him." She pulls me into a rough hug. "You're only a kitten – you shouldn't see dead bodies."

All through the play my mind spins. I'm dreading the end of the play – I'll have to tell Walter Mr Dale is dead and that I lost the statement and there's no chance of getting another.

The second the curtain comes down I leave to take Walter his food. I'm still wearing my costume. I really should have changed, but the longer I wait the harder it's going to be.

By the bridge, I catch sight of Valentina again. This time she's lurking in the shadows. She's looking back towards the theatre.

Who is she waiting for?

I look around for Captain Teach, but he's not out here.

I wait for ages. Eventually she steps out on to the cobbles and walks towards Narrow Quay. I weave through the Shambles and stop in the entrance of Wine Street.

Ambrose is there, outside a tavern. He's wearing a hooded cape, like someone who doesn't want to be seen, but I recognise his boots and I notice again how elegant his legs are. I dive into a doorway and lurk there. Two men come out of the tavern and all three cluster together, hiding in the deep shadow of the castle wall.

From my doorway I can't hear the men, but Ambrose's voice travels. Even his whispers are perfectly clear. "Here you go, my good fellows. A coin each for your efforts. This master of the boards is grateful. Very grateful. Good work." He bows slightly and scuttles off towards the river.

Perhaps that's it. Perhaps Ambrose is a killer, but he pays someone else to do it. Or he killed Lady Grey, and ran away with his elegant legs and red cloak, but these two killed Mr Dale?

It's completely possible.

I leave my hiding place and run down the street.

But why? Why would he want to kill a favourite to the queen?

He wouldn't, would he?

I'm clutching at straws.

Dread filling my stomach, I sneak the last few corners to the gaol.

"*I'll sing you one, O*," I murmur.

The white string drops from the window before I've even started the next line. I hook the basket on and it whizzes up the wall.

I stand back from the windows and call up. "Walter? Walter?"

Rattling echoes across the street and a pair of hands grip one of the bars of the highest window.

"Mouse? Thank you – I got the food."

"Food – food!" they all chant. "Have you brought us food, little mouse?" I try to ignore them. I really don't want to say what I need to say next.

"Walter, I've got bad news. Mr Dale, your witness, I'm afraid he's dead. I think he's been murdered!"

"Oh, that *is* bad news!" a voice shouts from somewhere off to the left.

"What?" says Walter. "No!"

"Don't worry though – I'm going to try and find who really did it," I shout, promising more than I can possibly deliver.

The whooping and shouting stills. Walter's voice comes out quiet and clear.

"Are you really going to try and track down a murderer?"

"I am," I mumble.

"Oh, Mouse, please don't. Please be careful."

"I'll be fine," I lie, thinking of Mr Dale. "Honestly."

"Begin with the blood, child," says a woman near my elbow. "Who has blood on them?"

"Blood! Blood! Blood!" they all chant.

Walter cries, "But what's to become of me?"

"You'll be walking up St Michael's Hill to the hanging tree soon enough," says a rasping voice.

The laughter stops and is replaced by low moans of agreement.

"Yup," says the woman from the cell below the ground. "If that little dolly on the other side of the road's your only help, you'll be up at the gallows in no time. Unless you can find out who done it, you're done for, matey."

Chapter 28

I worry all the way home.

I think I know who it is. And that terrifies me.

Could I set a trap with the blanket?

Could I, Mouse, catch them?

I've just promised Walter.

I feel the panic rise and rise in my chest.

But I have all the skills, don't I?

Or am I truly a mouse?

I'm sliding mouse-quiet through the lanes when I spot the two men that Ambrose was talking to earlier.

They're outside the same tavern, part of a small

group. I stop under an arch opposite, and wait to see if Ambrose appears. He doesn't, but I can hear their chatter.

"So that theatre bloke, he pays me—"

"He pays us!"

"He pays us — he pays us to cheer at his performance!"

"Free tickets an' all."

"What? How d'you get him to do that?" asks their friend.

"He just come in here and asked us straight out." The man holds the front of his jacket and does a full-on Ambrose. "'Noble saar,' he says. 'Noble saaar, could I prevail upon you to drum up some support at a forthcoming performance. I have need of your love and apro—' something."

"Or something like that," says the other. "Anyway, money for old rope if you ask me."

The man they're talking to is standing there open-mouthed.

I slip away. So that's what Ambrose has been up to — he's been paying for applause. That explains the sudden roars of approval when he comes on stage. Poor Ambrose — I never knew he was so desperate.

I leave through the arch and fiddle my way back through different streets.

It's not as if in my heart of hearts I didn't know.

Ambrose was always going to be innocent.

His heart's too kind.

A minute later I'm heading back towards the bridge when I become aware of footsteps behind me.

Lots of footsteps.

I break into a trot and the footsteps speed up.

I daren't look, but I think there must be three people. They're light, with pitter-pattery steps.

I duck down an alley.

"There she goes! Follow, lads!" It's a young voice, someone my age. And then I recognise them. It's the three boys I've run into before.

For a second I wonder if I should stay and fight – but this stupid dress won't help, and I've got nothing to fight with except my fists, and three against one isn't going to get me anywhere. And they probably have knives.

Grasping the skirts of the dress up around my hips, I break into a steady run.

They do too.

I'll head for the quay. There might be someone there to help.

But there isn't. For once, the quay is deserted. Running flat out, I weave through the piles of nets and rubbish on the harbourside. My pursuers fan out behind me.

I'm going to be trapped.

In front of me the water reflects moonlight. I've got no choice. I'll have to go in.

I kick off my boots.

But the dress…

Just before I leap, I undo the laces across the front of the dress. It begins to slip from my shoulders and as I plunge head first into the water it drags itself down my body. For a terrifying second it sticks on my hips, and then with two kicks I wriggle free and strike out for the far side.

"Whoa!" shouts one of the voices.

"Oh, lordy – she's drowned!" says another.

"Didn't mean for that to happen," says the third. "Only wanted her purse."

Letting my feet settle in the mud at the far side of the harbour I watch them reach into the water, trying to get to the dress. It's spread out across the surface and I suppose, in the dark, it might look as if there was someone still inside.

They make several attempts. One of them tries so hard he slips into the harbour and the other two have to pull him out.

"Let's go," says one.

"But there might be money there."

"Don't want to get done for murder," says another.

For about five minutes they stare into the water between the boats. Slowly, the dress absorbs all the water and sinks.

"She's gone."

"Get out of here."

"Shame," says another. "Expensive dress."

I wait with my nose sticking out of the water until I'm absolutely sure that they've gone. Things float past and the water's warm. I learned to swim here when I was little. It seemed cleaner then. A squeaking creature brushes my cheek. Water vole? Rat?

I don't think I can stay here any more, but my petticoat is white, and if I was vulnerable in a dress, I'm twice as obvious now.

Two wooden posts stick out from the shore. I bob over to them and haul myself up on the one nearest the theatre.

Then, as silent as I can, I run home, dripping.

Chapter 29

"And why are you all wet?" demands Valentina. She seems vexed.

I peel off my sopping petticoat. "Delivering food to Walter. Nobody else wants to do it."

"By water?"

"Set on, by boys," I say, rubbing myself dry with a length of sheet. "I ran. I should have fought them off."

I'm angry with myself for that.

And I'm angry with everyone else for leaving me to look after Walter.

And I'm cross at Mr Dale for dying and I'm furious

with myself for losing his testimony.

Underlying it all I'm scared.

But my anger's giving me courage.

"I can't have you doing this, Mouse," says Valentina, kissing the end of my nose. "You're too young to be sneaking around in the dark. And jumping into the river day or night is foolish."

I almost snap back that I've seen her sneaking about in the dark, but something stops me. Fear?

Prickles run down my spine.

It's her.

I know it is.

I gaze at her face. It's giving nothing away, just wrinkles on her forehead.

Dry-mouthed, I rasp, "With Mr Dale gone, the only way to save Walter is if I can prove that someone else did it."

Taking the sheet, she scrubs my hair with it. I want her to go away. I want to think, but she takes her time. When she's finished, she runs her fingernails softly over my back. "I don't think you should be poking your nose into murders. Sounds very dangerous –" she lands a kiss on my cheek; she smells of perfume and tar – "for a mousekin."

She's still standing behind me. I can feel her breath on my neck. "Don't mock me, Valentina," I bridle.

"Surely it's possible to find a murderer. Someone with blood on their hands. Someone with a reason to kill that woman. To kill Mr Dale."

"I suppose so," she says, taking a tiny bunch of my damp hair and dusting my ear with it, turning my head so that I'm looking into her wolfish eyes. "But how's a bobtail like you going to do that?" As I reach for my nightgown she whisks it out of my hands, dropping it down over my head so that I can't see her.

My heart's banging in my chest. My mouth's dry. I want to run, but I've got her here. I can ask. Can't I?

"I wondered if you could tell me anything about the murdered woman?" I say through the layers of cloth while struggling to find the armholes. "Lady Grey. Did you know her?"

There's a tiny pause. "Me? Goodness, no – just her name."

I push my head out of the neck hole and see that she's standing on the other side of the room, looking down at her hands.

"But didn't you have an idea who she was? You said something that day – like she was a favourite to the queen. So you knew *something* about her."

"Oh, did I?" Valentina catches her lower lip between her teeth and chews at it. "I don't remember that." She steps over to me, standing very close, and pulls my hair back so that it hurts and I have to pat her hand away.

"And you must have been talking to someone about getting the queen here. Was that her?"

I might be mistaken, but Valentina growls. I panic. I scrabble up on the hamper to my sleeping space, my back to the wall. She follows and kneels looking out of my window, as if the moon is very interesting.

I'm trapped.

The air is heavy and still between us. I want her to go.

I want her to stay.

Valentina picks up my coverlet, pinching it between thumb and forefinger, and drops it again so that it lands skewed. For a moment her cool eyes seem colder than the grave.

"Beware of meddling where you shouldn't, Mouse."

There's a huge empty silence. We stare eye to eye. The breathless silence stretches to fill the room. Time halts. My head prickles, scalp to shoulders and back again.

Until she breaks it by suddenly reaching under my mattress, all jolly and cheerful and oddly normal.

"Oh! What's that under your bed?"

"What?" I say, a stupid blush rising from my chest.

"Why have you got this grubby old blanket?" She pulls the blanket out and bundles it in her arms. "How horrible, it's got something on it. I'll give it a wash."

"Don't worry, I'll do it. I found it. I thought Dog could sleep on it."

"I'll wash it first. Don't want you getting filthy, poppet. Night, lambkin."

"But, Valentina!"

"Not a problem, Mouseling – I'll do it."

I hear her squeak down the hampers humming to herself. I listen to her talking to her little bird. I hear it flutter back and forth in the tiny cage.

I lie in the gloom under my coverlet, gazing up. My carved figures stare back at me, dancing in the candlelight.

I turn over and lie on my side. Without Dog on my legs it's hard to sleep.

And my brain's galloping.

I've challenged her.

And now she's threatening me.

Chapter 30

I barely sleep, but in the morning the chill of last night has gone and Valentina's all smiles.

For a moment, I doubt myself and fill my head with reasonable explanations.

She might genuinely be worried about me having a skanky old blanket. Mr Dale's testimony might have blown out of the window.

She might have been looking out for me last night. She might actually be worried for my safety.

But almost immediately, my neck is prickling. I'm seeing through her words.

"I want you to do me a favour, little bunny. Get

something – something secret – for me."

I turn on to my elbow so that I can look down at her.

The distance between us feels huge. Is that what happens when you lose trust?

"What secret thing?"

She eyes me for a moment. "Do I sense reluctance, poppet?"

I don't reply.

"Ah," she says. "You're wondering about Walter, aren't you? You're wondering if my errand is going to help him get out of prison. Whether my little plan will make any difference." She goes up on her tiptoes and pulls me closer until her nose almost meets mine. "You're wondering – what I'm up to?"

I don't move my head, I simply stare.

"Well, little Mouse." She sits on the side of my bed, watching a spider in my window wrapping a fly in silk. Turning it into dinner. "My plan is simple." A look of concern crosses her face. "I can't magically conjure another witness, or find out who actually murdered the woman – I have no idea how to – but I feel sure we can get a pardon."

"A pardon? Who from?"

"From the queen."

That's it. It's all about the queen. I think of

Valentina's grand connections, her grand ways, her trips abroad. Her languages. It all makes sense. She wants to get to the queen.

I make the fastest of decisions. I will play along. I will stay close to Valentina. I will pretend.

"I told you, Mouse, we're famous. So famous that the queen has said she'd love to come here and play a leading role in a performance."

I sit with my mouth open. I hope I look massively impressed. "She's going to act with us?"

"Yes. And when she comes, you could ask her for a pardon."

"Oh! That's wonderful." I clap my hands together. Perhaps that's overdoing it, so I moderate the joy and narrow my eyes. "So why the secret thing?"

I sense that Valentina is irritated by my questions but that she's determined not to show it. She nibbles the skin by her thumbnail, tearing a tiny shred with her teeth. "The secret thing is a potion. A very, very expensive potion. Rare beyond..." She waves her hands in a snake motion. "From the East."

"And what does it do?"

She looks at me hard. As if she's measuring my ability to keep a secret. "It makes anyone who receives it do the bidding of the person in front of them. It doesn't last long and it's illegal – you're not allowed to use it, for obvious reasons — but used with subtlety…"

I gasp, widen my eyes and say, "You mean, if we gave her some, the queen would *have* to sign the pardon?"

"Yes. You in?"

I nod. "Of course. How do I get this stuff?"

"It's at the Golden Sheaf. It's an ale house — out beyond Redcliffe. You'll have to dress as a boy, it'll be safer. I'll give you these." She drops three gold coins into my palm. "I've already paid half. The place is run by a woman. Tell her you've come from Mary."

"Who's Mary?"

"I am — or at least, that's the name I gave." Valentina flashes a tiny tight smile. "You'll give her some money, and she'll give you a bottle. Let no one see you. Bring it back to me. I'll cover for you — tell them you're getting some make-up for me." She holds my hand tight for a second, her silver eyes looking into mine. I hold her gaze. "Good luck, Mouse."

Chapter 31

I pause in the shade below the gallery and drag my thoughts together. I have to go. I have to get the potion. I have to bring something back for Valentina. She'll know otherwise. For now, she needs to think I haven't worked it out, even though she must know I suspect something.

But I have to make sure that she doesn't give whatever it is to the queen. I'm not so gullible as to think it's possible to make anyone do your bidding with a potion. If such a thing existed, I'd have heard of it.

All of this explains the murders.

First, the woman on the quayside, who must have rumbled Valentina. She must have been the connection to the queen.

Second, Mr Dale, who must have seen Valentina. A tall man, running from the scene. Wearing the red cape. The bloodstained blanket.

He might have been killed by Valentina. Or Captain Teach.

That would explain her passing him money.

But why would she want to get to the queen?

I stare up at a bird circling overhead.

She doesn't want to do anything good. I'm sure of that.

I think back to the conversation I overheard between Jameson and Stuart. They were talking about a duke from the continent – how he'd got spies in every town. How he was rumoured to have employed an assassin to kill the queen.

An assassin?

I take a couple of deep breaths.

I shouldn't be doing this.

But I have to.

I wish I could take Dog in case of trouble. Not that he'd do much more than bark, but he might scare someone off. From the description that Valentina gave, the inn is quite a way out of town. There are plenty of cutpurses between here and the countryside.

Checking my reflection in one of the mirrored lanterns, I cram my hair under my hat and decide that I look more boy than girl. I don't want a repeat of last night. Bridget's already poking around looking at dresses like she's noticed one's missing.

I take a moment to look for the red blanket but I can't see it anywhere. Not even drying on the washing line.

"Where are you sneaking off to then?" asks Eve, calling to me as I'm about to go out through the big doors.

"None of your business," I say, pulling up the bar that bolts the doors.

She jumps lightly from the gallery and poses in an arabesque, her soft little arms forming a perfect curve above her head. "But I want to know."

Ignoring her, I slam the big door shut behind me.

"Do you want Dog back?" she shouts through it.

For a second I pause. No. I'm not going to let it show. I'm really not. She can keep Dog until she tires of him. If she thinks it's hurting me then she'll never let him go.

At least, that's what I tell myself.

Turning away from the theatre, I pick my way over the crusted mud that surrounds the Moth.

"Can I come?" asks a voice behind me.

It's Adam. He's standing on a tussock a few paces behind me.

"What?"

"Can I come wherever it is you're going?"

I shake my head and jump over the ruts of the mud, moving faster than I intended.

"Please, Mouse. I want to be your friend." He runs alongside me. "Please."

There's something desperate in his tone. But, "No," I say. "No, you can't come with me. And honestly? You've had years to be my friend – you can't just decide to do it now."

"But, Mouse, I'm not like her. And the thing with Dog – it's just mean."

I stop and he stops. We stare at each other. He actually looks as if he wants to be my friend.

I look at him and he looks at the ground. "She's foul. I know she is. She's complete poison. And I know, and Ma knows, that you're kind and lovely, and that Eve's ... a monster. But Pa's besotted. He can't see the real Eve, because he doesn't want to. And because we're brother and sister, everyone thinks I'm as bad as she is, but I'm not. I'm really not like her. And I know I backed her up the other day – and I shouldn't have done – but, please, Mouse. Give me a chance. Let me be your friend."

His cheeks are burning and a second later a torrent of tears pours down them. Very convincing tears, but he is an actor.

Adam and I are very much alone in the sea of dried mud crusts.

"I don't know, Adam. I don't know – and I'm sorry, but you can't come with me. Not today anyway."

I turn and jog away from him, listening out for his footsteps, but they don't come. When I reach the warehouse, I look back. Adam is standing where I left him, looking down at his feet. The tears are still pouring down his face.

Chapter 32

Feeling confused, I walk through the lanes, past the early-morning market traders pushing hand barrows of vegetables towards the bridge. Despite the hour, groups of people hang around the inns chattering and shouting and stumbling into the street.

I wonder about everything and everyone.

A week ago, my world was solid and safe. I'd have known who was an enemy and who was a friend.

I'd have put Valentina in the friends.

And Adam in the enemies.

But the world's turned upside down.

I've known Adam and his sister since I can remember.

She's younger than me and he's younger than her. In the beginning the three of us played together. Walter and Mrs Hawkin gave us sticks and hoops to run with. We built little models of the theatre and performed plays to each other. Most nights we slept together in a bundle, like puppies. We built dens in the costume hampers. We made dolls from the scraps. When it rained and we were stuck inside, Walter sang songs. Before we went to sleep, we listened to Kwadwo's stories of pythons and giant spiders, or fell asleep in seconds to Mr Hawkin's recitations of a tedious Latin poem. When it was Valentina's turn, she acted out tales of heroism and tragedy. Some of them were brutal. I remember Mrs Hawkin coming over to our bed and exclaiming with horror because Valentina had been acting out a tale in which someone gets tricked into eating their own children in a pie. Although we were in our nightclothes, she'd daubed us in stage blood. Eve was rapt. I'm not sure I understood then, but something altered at that point. Eve changed from irritating to something else, something more calculated. Whatever it was, I no longer spent time with Eve and Adam. Instead I was alone with Walter until I was old enough to be treated as a member of the theatre and began to learn the arts I would need to survive. I had Kwadwo, Walter and Valentina as my teachers. They had Mr and Mrs Hawkin.

Valentina still told me bedtime stories. Most of them ended in death. But then most of the plays we perform end in death, for me, or Walter, or Valentina, or all of us.

Pausing for a moment, I look back. I can still see the theatre over the warehouses. Thinking about it, I could have gone on playing with Adam. I wonder why we stopped. Perhaps it was the age gap. I was learning sword fighting and he was still playing in the clay.

Or perhaps it was Mrs Hawkin seeing Valentina for what she is.

Perhaps Adam's right; perhaps we could be friends now. I should have been kinder to him.

I'll try when I get back.

I stomp through the chattering streets into the emptier ones that lie around the edges of the city. There are workshops and warehouses here, hanging doors that creak in the wind and none of the streets have names. I walk uphill, away from the river, past small fields and farms. The strong smell of cows and the soft sound of chewing floats over the stone walls, and ripe plums hang over the lane. I fill my cheeks with them, spitting stones back over into the fields.

An hour into the walk, a daywalker fox trots

across my path and I know that I'm properly in the countryside now. Fat-fruited brambles tumble over fences, tall heads of foxglove seeds clatter above my head and the houses get further apart. Some of them are busy with washing and hens and people, others barely fit for a human.

The fields smell of straw and pigs and hay.

I walk on, passing an ancient woman pulling a plough over her stony patch. A dead badger that smells extraordinary. Eventually the lane widens and under a group of chestnut trees I see a muddle of dark houses, some with their shutters open, some blank.

I'd imagined the Golden Sheaf as a cosy, welcoming place, but it turns out to be a broken building, once thatched, now bald. Someone's drawn a crude picture of a straw stook on a board and it stands outside by the gate surrounded by tall downy thistles. If I hadn't been looking so hard, I wouldn't have found it.

A worn path through the undergrowth leads to the dark doorway.

I stand in the lane for a minute, staring. If I don't come back no one will ever know.

I adopt a boy swagger, swinging my feet and my shoulders more than needed. I haven't even opened the gate when feet sound on the stairs inside and a woman opens the door. As she looks at me, I look at her. Or

I try to. Her face is dark with tattoos. Every scrap of it is marked, some of it black, some of it faded blue-green like the sailors that come into the theatre. And like some of the tattoos that the sailors have, there are monsters. Squid and fish and things that crawl in the mud of the estuary mixing madly with clouds and cherubs. Her eyes are dark but her hair is a mess of white froth, and snow white. Stage characters included, she's the strangest person I've ever seen.

"What are you here for?" she whispers from the doorway.

"Mary sent me." I speak in my lowest voice. It's not convincing. I shouldn't have done that. I should have gone for high like I do on the stage.

"Mary? She sent you?"

"That's what I said." I let my voice drift a little higher.

A flicker of something crosses her features. It might be surprise. It might be disappointment. But she stands back and beckons me in.

Chapter 33

"You're early, but come inside," she says, ushering me through the doorway into a room where the walls are lined with jars and the air's thick with something burning. "Camphor," she says. "To keep the insects away."

"I didn't know there was a time — sorry."

"No matter." She goes to the window and arranges a red scarf there behind the glass. It strikes me as strange but I'm not going to challenge her. "Mary, eh?" She laughs a pretty bell laugh. "This is what she ordered." She unlocks a chest, reaches in and brings out two tiny blue bottles with no labels. She places them on the table between us, keeping her fingers on the corked tops.

"Two? How do I know what it is?" I ask peering at them. "Are there any instructions?"

"It's what she asked for ... and she knows what to do."

I reach out for the bottles, but she keeps her fingers on the tops.

"Did she give you the money?" she says, looking past my shoulder to the door.

"Here." I place the gold coins in the dust on the table. She raises an eyebrow and the octopus on her head raises a tentacle. "That's right, isn't it?" I say, looking up at her. Now the octopus is flicking. Pulsing. My eyes keep on drifting towards it. It's as if her skin's alive.

"Why did Mary not come herself?" she asks.

I hesitate. "I don't know."

"What's your name?"

"Mine?"

"Yes – what are you called?"

"Tom," I answer quickly.

"Really?" she says, moving closer to me so that I can really see that octopus flailing around. "You don't look like a Tom. I wonder – if I called 'Tom' across a room, would you answer?"

I smile and pull my hat a little lower.

Again, she looks past me towards the doorway.

"Would you like a drink? You've come such a long way. I could give you something warm to go home with?"

I glance around at the bottles and the jars. Some of them have white shapes inside, dead things. Vegetable and animal. None of them look as if I'd want to drink them.

She laughs. "Don't worry – not in here. This is my workshop. I have a kitchen, with chocolate and sugar and tasty treats. I could make you something delicious."

"Oh, no – thank you. I should get back."

"I have some little rabbits at the back. Would you like to see them? They're very sweet." She lets go of the bottles and moves towards a curtain that hangs over a doorway behind her.

"Oh, no," I say, grabbing the bottles from the tabletop and jamming them in my pocket. "Thank you – I've got what I came for."

"But you should—"

"I have to get home, thank you," I say, backing towards the door.

She stares at me. This time her face behind the octopus forms a slow frown, and I turn to grab the door handle.

"Wait!" she calls, but I'm spooked and I'm not staying a second more in a room full of dead things with an angry octopus woman. "Tom!" she shouts, but she's right. I don't answer to that name.

Something crashes to the ground and in the corner of my vision I see two figures emerge from a shed across the lane.

They're moving very fast towards me.

Chapter 34

I don't wait; I don't look.

Behind me, the woman's shouting something at them. It sounds like encouragement.

I speed up, charging down the path and on to the lane so that I swing back towards the city. I know I can run. I know I can run faster than Eve or Adam, or those scary city boys for a short time. But this is different. I've never been chased like this. I don't know if I can outstrip these two. It's daylight and there's no water to throw myself into.

Their feet thunder closer. Heavy breathing. They can almost grab me.

Panic fills my lungs; my feet grow wings. Filled with sudden energy, I leap from tussock to tussock, stone to stone, leaning forward and powering away from the house. I jump across the corner of the lane, vaulting over two stone walls to cut away a few paces of running and I let myself smile as I hear one of the men attempting to do the same and failing.

"What d'you do that for, you idiot?" shouts the other, who sounds further away.

Familiar voices?

Stumbling over the uneven ground, I try to get a lead on them, but the ground is so lumpy I can't run like I want to. All I can do is try.

A farmyard opens up on the right and we pass a shed that smells of sour milk. I dive off the lane and race around the back of the building, skipping over a low wall on the far side. I hear them shout directions at each other and I buy myself another second leading them off through an orchard full of goats, but once I'm back on the lane they seem to speed up.

With every stride I'm looking for a way out, a turn. We pass a hayrick and I wonder if I could hide inside, but they're too close and I'd be caught like a rat so I keep leaping and bounding until I reach cobbles.

With the ground hard under my feet I run flat out, my lungs bellowing in and out. It's mostly downhill and I love the twists and turns of the lane. They're easier for me than for them and I can hear blundering and crashing behind me.

Good.

Ahead of me, Redcliffe Tower gives me an easy target to aim for. Behind me, the men are wheezing, and judging by the rhythm of their feet, one of them might be lame.

Lines of cottages now flank the road. Three small boys charge out in front of me, kicking a stone into the lane, I dodge through but I hear one of the men swear and stumble.

I tear on, not daring to let up one little bit. The roads are becoming familiar. I don't want to lead them back to the theatre. I swing over to the right, towards the Temple Church. Their pounding feet follow.

Veering back to the left, I dive down a narrow street that I know has a bakery where there'll be a queue. The smell of the bread's brought a crowd. A group of women stand clustered around the entrance, each carrying a basket, each with skirts and children clinging to them.

"Sorry!" I mutter, leaping past the skirts and brushing a toddler.

"'Ere! Watch your step!" shouts one.

"Get off!" shouts another.

But I'm past, and I'm heading for the bridge.

Behind me, the men cannon into the queue and their voices fade a little and my heart lifts as ahead of me I can see the masts of the tall ships. Not far to the harbour, which has plenty of places to hide, but my sides are aching and my feet sting from slapping on the cobbles. I can't keep this up.

I throw myself into the masses fighting to get over the bridge. I can't run any more, but then the men can't either and with a market setting off along the Shambles it's going to be impossible to see me.

I hope.

Once I'm on the other side, I break into a jog, avoiding the crowds and dodging down towards the inns at the quayside. They're rough places, but I think I can risk it in the daytime. I get to the Backs and duck in through the middle door of the Llandoger Trow. It's a massive inn and it's crammed with sailors and scary men and hooting women. Smoke belches from a huge fireplace and the air's so thick with sweat and spirits that it almost takes my breath away.

I slink through the wild crowd to the back. "Hey!" someone shouts as I tunnel through, pushing under the tankards, over the unconscious and out into the small barrel-filled yard at the back. It's surrounded by high walls. There are three small kegs in a row on the ground. Fast as I can, I stack them on top of each other and scramble up, clearing the wall and kicking the barrels over as I go. On the other side I land badly and I limp over to the shade of a scrubby tree to recover.

I don't know for sure if the men followed me in. And if they did, will they work out where I went? They might have lost sight earlier, but I want to actually see them. I look up. The tree is an easy climb and there's plenty of thick foliage to hide inside. From a branch near the top, it's possible to see over the wall, so I balance up there, waiting. It takes a while but eventually two men trailing a cloud of flies come out into the yard. I hear them move the barrels. They pick them up, shake them, put them down. They don't say anything for ages and I only get glimpses of their heads. One of them is much taller than the other and by hanging off the branch I get a good view of his hair that sticks straight up, short and thick. He's young, and yes, I do know him. Stuart. I try to get a look at the other man, but he's so much shorter.

It must be Jameson.

Crawling out along the branch to the bendiest tip, I risk a good long stare.

"So where is he?" says Stuart.

"She — that wasn't a 'he'. Over the wall, I imagine."

Stuart sighs. "We're not going to find her now. It's a warren."

"That woman put the signal up – we had plenty of time."

"Yes, but that little stoat was far too fast. We didn't stand a chance."

"I don't honestly care. I've not run that far or that fast for too many years." The speaker leans forward and coughs until something comes up.

I hear the spit hit the ground.

"Drink? We deserve it."

And then they give up, slapping each other on the back, and head back inside to join the drinkers.

Dropping down from the tree, I slip my fingers around the bottles. They were supposed to catch me.

Did Valentina tell them?

I turn the bottles over in my pocket. They must be something incriminating.

Something that would really get me in trouble.

And, after all, who'd believe an orphan from the theatre over a leading lady?

Chapter 35

I hurry back over the bridge and thump straight into the crowds of people cramming in through the theatre doors. Since Walter was arrested, we've had much bigger audiences. It's the notoriety, I guess.

Keeping my head low, I shove past the drunks. Inside, despite the open roof, the air is thick with breath and sweat. All around the sides are people selling food, tobacco and cider. Their calls mingle with the crowd and, bottled up in the confines of the theatre, it's loud.

I thread my way through the legs until I can access the curtain to the wings.

Backstage, the company is gathered in a circle, Mr Hawkin in the middle. Bridget's staring at him open-mouthed.

"You may well stand shocked and surprised, but yes, Her Majesty *is* coming and we must prepare! Put out the flags, unfurl the pennants, polish the brass – raise high the roof beams, carpenters. Here comes the bride, to paraphrase the great Sappho!" He waves his arms to show the shambolic costume room. "All this we must mend, buff, dust, clean! All of it must be fixed. Immediately! Friends, comrades, allies – we must break out the saws and hammers, the paint pots and brushes, the brooms and cloths, the buckets, the—"

"This cannot possibly be true. Can it?" asks Ambrose of Valentina, who is sitting at the make-up table dotting her chin with charcoal.

"It is," she says. "Cross my heart."

Everyone begins to talk at once and Valentina looks back into her mirror, spotting me over her shoulder. "Oh!" she says, eyes wide before she quickly makes them smile. "You made it?"

"I did," I say, gripping the bottles in my fist. "So the secret's out then?"

"It is. I had to tell Mr H. Do I look like a man?" She pauses, meeting my gaze in the mirror. "How did it go?"

I hold out the little bottles in the palm of my hand but close my fingers around them straight away.

"Oh, well done, poppet. And well done for getting back safely."

"Those men followed me. Jameson and Stewart."

She turns to look at me for the first time. "But they didn't catch you, bunny?" Her eyes are wide as she asks me the question.

"No, they didn't."

"Clever Mouse," she says, puffing powder over her face. "I knew you'd be good at it."

"But it was like they were expecting me."

"Was it? Lucky you're a fast runner. Now, leave the bottles on my bed, then help me on with this jacket and get yourself into your costume. Our plan is coming together and getting me the potion is quite wonderful. Thank you, Mouse. You've no idea how helpful you are."

Before I put on my costume, I pour the contents of the bottles out of my window and replace them with sugar water, finally leaving them on Valentina's coverlet. I don't know what Valentina sent me for but it definitely wasn't a magical potion. My guess is that it was poison. And that I was either to be caught buying it, or she would end up with a handy bottle to use later.

Either way she'd win.

I run downstairs to find Bridget trying to light a candle for a lantern. "Honestly, this paper won't light at all." She holds up a lightly singed spill.

I grab another from the mantlepiece, but it's thicker than normal and feels different. I unfold it, and through the twists I read the remains of Mr Dale's handwriting.

I hand Bridget a lit straw and knock the ash from the end of the spill she's been holding.

I unfurl them all, but there are only fragments of Mr Dale's statement. None of them are useful, all of them are singed and one of them has grey mud on it.

Useless, but final proof of something.

As if I needed it.

Carefully, I tuck them behind a mirror. If I only had the blanket. Together with the tapers, they'd be proper evidence.

Bridget looks at me. "Happy, are you? Rustling around in there like a mouse? Oh this blessed dress – how's a body supposed to put this kind of thing on?" She stands in her petticoat with the dress around her ankles, picking at the mess of laces and embroidery.

"I'll help," I say.

"We shouldn't be doing this queen thing," she says as I haul in the laces of her stays and settle the peplum around her hips. "We're a little provincial theatre company — more bawd than bard — and we shouldn't be reaching above our station." She throws powder on to her sweating cheeks. "What possessed Valentina to even think of such a thing?"

Murder, I think to myself. She is possessed by murder.

Once I've squeezed Bridget into her costume, I have to wriggle into mine. It's one that was made when I was shorter. I can barely move my shoulders but I shuffle out to join the others. It's a different play tonight. A comedy, and Adam, Eve and I play putti — they're the cherubs that blow winds, and mess about in the corners of paintings, except that we do it on the stage. According to Mr Hawkin, it gives us an "Italian verisimilitude". Valentina is playing a man who dresses as a girl, who dresses as a man. Her changes take so long, we need to spend as much time as we can "amusing the audience with our antics".

There's a tightrope set up high over the stage, which Kwadwo usually checks, but tonight he's busy hauling the scenery up and down.

"It's all fine," says Eve to her father. "I've checked it. It's perfectly good."

"What?" I say, but Mr Hawkin ushers me over to Adam to get into my wings. "Buckle up, Mouse, buckle up. Wings for all today."

My heart beating at twice the normal speed, I struggle into the harness and help Adam into his.

"Cheer up!" says Ambrose, picking up his violin and shoving us on to the stage.

The idea is that while Adam and Eve roll over each other and wrap each other in lengths of silk, I walk over their heads on the tightrope. I've done it a thousand times but as we go on stage, Eve gives me one of her smiles.

I glance back at the sash tied around one of the great pillars that holds up the roof. It looks all right from here but the one on the other side is hidden behind the ladder I climb to get up there.

Ambrose plays a jaunty jig and the audience go wild for him, yelling and clapping as if they've never seen him before. As he plays, Eve bobs into the middle of the stage, pulling curtsies. Adam bows and I stare up at the rope.

They link hands and begin to do the roll thing. One of Adam's wings is torn off by a nail sticking out of the front of the stage and the crowd yowls with laughter. I launch myself over, somersaulting across the stage behind them, and reach the ladder.

I do a load of fancy poses as I climb the ladder to get a good look at the way the rope is tied.

But it looks secure. The right knot.

The tune of the fiddle changes from cheery to mournful and the crowd standing near the stage slap their palms on the wood so that the whole theatre reverberates.

Adam and Eve stop rolling around and stand back, their arms up towards me, and the audience goes quiet.

Perching at the top of the ladder, I look along the rope. It looks ordinary, just as it should. I glance down to Eve. She's smiling up at me. "Go on," she whispers.

The audience begin a slow handclap. Ambrose glares at me and I hear Mr Hawkin muttering in the wings behind me, "Hurry up, child!"

Doing all the graceful things with my arms, I take a firm pace forward. The rope holds. I arch over and place one hand on the rope, lifting the rest of my body into the air, and the crowd *oohs*. When I land with both feet on the far side, they *aah*.

Perhaps I'm imagining things.

Flip-flopping my way along the white line, I focus on keeping my body on the right plane, my muscles still, no wobble, and it's all going well until I spot the fray. Two frays. Someone has cut my rope and it's stretching.

Maybe I could dance over the rest and get to the end. Or I could jump off and land on the stage. I stand on one foot and give myself a moment to think. The rope suddenly sags, wobbling, and I'm forced to put my arms out on both sides to steady myself.

"*OOOH!*" roars the crowd.

"Lost your nerve, girl?" shouts a man.

Darting a smile at the audience I lean forward and grasp the rope with both hands, fingers either side of the slash. Then, much sooner than I should, I launch my feet in the air, twist twice and somersault on to the ground. I bow, and as I do, the two pieces of the rope fall heavily to the stage.

"OOOOH!" A huge roar from the crowd and cries of "*Brava*" from the wings.

I look up. Adam is standing open-mouthed, staring at the broken rope, but Eve has all the clouds of Hell settled in a band across her forehead.

Chapter 36

When the audience has gone and everyone else is upstairs getting changed out of their costumes, Mrs Hawkin sits on the stage with the two ends of the rope in her hands and stares at her daughter. Although I was the victim, it feels as though Mrs Hawkin is taking it personally. Eve stares at the ground and pokes the rope with her toe. "I couldn't have possibly done it, Mama. Mouse must have done it."

"And why?" says her mother, wiping the back of her hand over her brow and sweeping her unruly hair back to the top of her head. "Why on earth would Mouse attack herself?"

Eve shrugs. Her bottom lip is stuck firm in a pout and her eyes are fixed downwards.

"It makes no sense, child." She gives her daughter time to speak and I step back into the shadows. I don't feel threatened by Eve, even though she's trying to hurt me. It feels like she's lashing out because she wants to prove something. To me? To someone else?

"Well, there'll be no more of it," says Mrs Hawkin. "Now, apologise to Mouse."

"Do I have to?" says Eve.

Mrs Hawkin gives her a shove in my direction. I don't really want Eve to apologise, I want her to disappear, but we go through an uncomfortable moment in which she mumbles a few words she doesn't believe and I, not believing her, accept them.

After the apology, Mrs Hawkin kisses us both on our heads, holding us close to her chest, so that we're face to face. "I love you, Eve," she says, and Eve's face glows, a soft smile – a proper happy one – playing over her lips. "And I love you too, Mouse. I love you as my own." That's when Eve's face crumples. Not completely, not bawling tears, but it creases up and for a moment I see the baby behind the face.

"Dog must go back to Mouse now, Eve – it's not fair on either of them."

Eve sniffs and I feel the slightest sense of victory

tempered with something like regret — or sadness; I can't quite put my finger on it.

When Mrs Hawkin releases us, I go up and change. Bridget has gone and Valentina and Ambrose are having a snippy row about the queen. For once, their voices don't carry and I'm left wondering if Ambrose has come to the same conclusion as me.

I'll talk to him tomorrow if I can, but just now I need to take Walter his food.

Chapter 37

First thing in the morning, seeing that Valentina's asleep, I scuttle down to Kwadwo.

He hands me a bowl of hot spiced apple and mulberry, and a sweet roll to dip in it.

"Mouse, do you ever use the furnace at the back of the theatre?"

I shake my head.

He chops a bulb of onion and my eyes water from the gas. "Why?" I ask.

He shakes his head and looks up, but not at me, and then looks down at the onion again. "I found something in the furnace," he says. "Or a bit of something. Over there — on the table. It's odd, because I've never found anything that I haven't put in there. Ever."

I stand and walk over to a table piled high with books, spices, leather, feathers, so much stuff I can't spot what he means.

"In the corner." He wipes his forehead against his upper arm and points. "See?"

I pick it up. It's a strip of singed fabric, half burned, the remnants of a larger garment. It's red. Wool.

"Do you know what it is?" he asks, moving towards me and gazing at the fabric. "Is someone else using our furnace, perhaps?"

"I know what it is," I say, sickness adding to the dread already in my stomach. "And I know who put it there."

"What is it, Mouse?" Kwadwo rubs the cloth between his fingers. "What's the matter? What's going on?"

I look at his long fingers holding the red cloth and I'm burning to tell him about Valentina.

But then I think about his position. If he thought I was at risk in any way, he'd stand up for me. He'd make a fuss. He'd stand up to Valentina, risk his life. Or he'd go to Stuart and Jameson. He'd do that, and he'd lose his freedom.

Or worse. His life.

"I don't know, I don't know," I say, dropping the cloth back on the table. "It's probably nothing."

I can feel his eyes on my back as I leave. But I just can't tell him.

I meet Valentina on the stairs and pull a grin I don't feel into place.

"Mouseling!" She spins me round, one way then the other. I want to shout, to push her away. I want to run to Mrs Hawkin, Bridget – anyone – but instead I giggle.

She's wearing an orange silk dress and her hair is in ringlets. She looks grander than when she's on stage, and there's a buzz coming off her. All titters and excitement.

"Let's dress up again," she says. "Look – I've brought you breakfast." She hands me a sticky raisin bun that seems fresh. She must have been into the town already to get it. I put it in my pocket for later.

"Now, how about the green velvet? You look lovely in that." She crawls up into my space and begins to fluff through my clothes. "We'll go into town, take tea somewhere."

"But I don't want to come. I want to stay here."

Valentina pauses. She settles her wolf eyes on me.

"Duckling?"

Immediately regretting my refusal, I shrug. "It's just … I've got Dog back and I want to spend time with him. And I don't feel like dressing up."

She raises an eyebrow. She glances up at the heart I've carved around Walter.

"He may not come back, you know," she says in a sharp voice, like Eve's.

I swallow.

She huffs, picking up a stack of fresh paper and a bottle of ink. "Well, I'm not going to hang around here with a mouseling. I'm off out, to write a play and enjoy myself."

As she leaves, I run to the front of the dressing room and look down on the stage. Eve is sitting there with her legs crossed. She looks like a small child.

As Valentina passes, Eve looks up at her with the sweetest, softest smile. Not at all like the smile she gave her mother last night. This is different. This is absolute love and I realise that she adores Valentina. Is this what the rope trick was about? To prove to Valentina that she can outwit me? That *she* is talent?

"Can I come with you, please, Valentina?"

There's a pause while Valentina looks at Eve — almost studies her — and then turns on her heel.

"No," says Valentina, leaving the theatre.

Chapter 38

I stood up to Valentina, and as a result I have no idea where she's been all afternoon. And I have no idea what to do about her. At least nobody else has died, although Ambrose worries me by missing the start of the play.

"Drunk, I imagine," says Mr Hawkin. "I shall play his part."

When eventually Ambrose does arrive, he and Valentina argue again.

He comes over to me, as if he wants to ask me something, but she heads me off, sending me to pick up her little bird from the windowsill in her sleeping space.

The bird looks somehow battered, and when I pick it up, it throws itself against the bars.

"S'all right, little thing," I say, but it goes on flapping in the tiny space, even after I've brought it down to the make-up table.

When I look around for Ambrose, he's already going on stage.

Dog trots over and sits by my feet. I reach down and sink my fingers into the thick fur around his neck. He rumbles his approval. I bury my nose in his coat and breathe him in.

"You doing all right there, Mouse?" asks Valentina, pinning her hat to her hair. She's a murdered woman in tonight's play and she's already covered in blood. I can't help thinking it belongs to someone.

"Yes," I say. Although I'm not, and I almost miss my entrance because I'm watching her calmly wipe the blood from her hands on to a rag. I can't help it; I'm now watching everything she does. I don't know if it's worse if she's under my nose or when I can't see her.

A moment later Bridget rushes backstage and wipes stage blood from a dagger on to the same rag.

My head buzzes.

Chapter 39

By the end of the play I've exhausted myself just worrying, but Walter still needs his food.

"I could take it," says Kwadwo. "You're so tired."

"No," I say. "I'll do it."

I leave, but I wait in the shadow of the largest warehouse. I watch Valentina leave. And then a moment later Ambrose follows her. They both go over the bridge, but when she pauses, he stops, looking into the river as if there's something really interesting down there.

I rush to get to him, but he's too far ahead and slips quietly into the shadows of the boats on the far side of the river.

I'll have to talk to him tomorrow. For now, I'll go to Walter.

When I reach the prison, he gets the food and I have nothing hopeful to say, so I say nothing.

Chapter 40

My sickness grows as I walk back to the theatre.

I look into Valentina's space. The bird's sitting quietly on the bottom of the cage. Its wings are droopy. It looks like a plant that's not been watered.

I pour some water into an egg cup and slip it in through the doorway.

The bird drinks, long and deep.

Surely even Valentina knows that birds need water?

I lie awake under the boards, listening for her return.

Hours later I hear her creep in and wash in a basin.

Chapter 11

I wake before it's light. Even before the seagulls. Pulling on trousers, I slip down from my bed and tiptoe past Valentina and out of the costume store.

Kwadwo is repairing the gallery rails.

"You're early," he says.

I hesitate. I so want to tell him everything. But no, I mustn't.

"I am," I say, breezily pushing open the large doors of the theatre and peering out across the baked earth outside.

Nothing seems different, but I can't help feeling that something's up. Whistling Dog to my side, I wander over towards the bridge. Then I spot the small crowd of people collecting on the other side of the river.

They're not completely silent, but they are unusually quiet.

Dog and I trot past the warehouses and stop on the top of the bridge. From here I can see past the ships and their cargos to the people gathered. They seem to be clustered around something at their feet. Someone turns away to spit into the harbour and I get a glimpse of a body on the ground.

"C'mon, Dog," I say, and we trot along the quayside, dodging the sea rubbish heaped along the path. The group has closed up again and I have to force my way between two pungent sailors so that I can see what they're looking at.

I wish I hadn't.

There, curled on his side, a thin line of blood from his ear across to a pool that has formed by the stones of the quay, is Ambrose.

Chapter 42

I run back to the theatre in shock. Before I've thought about it I'm yelling for Valentina.

"Ambrose – he's dead – he's been killed!" I shake her shoulder. "Wake up!"

She turns over and faces the wall. "What is it, Mouse?" she mumbles. "It's so early, do pipe down."

"Wake up!"

She doesn't move but I keep talking.

"He's on the quayside. Someone's killed him."

"Who?" she mutters.

"Ambrose – someone's killed him."

She rolls over on to her back and reaches up to

me, pulling me down into her hair. She smells as she always does, of perfume and candles and something else. Something mannish. Her arms are tight around me. Holding me like Walter would.

"Oh dear." Rubbing her chin on my shoulder. "That's a shame, but there there, little mouse. It'll be OK."

"But how can it be fine?" I splutter. "Ambrose. Our Ambrose is dead! You don't seem at all surprised."

There's a long pause while Valentina looks at her hand against the light and I imagine her creeping up on Ambrose and killing him. Slipping something in his ear.

She couldn't. Could she?

She seems to weigh something up in her head. "I'm sorry about Ambrose, of course I am. He was a dear, sweet man. Pompous and self-important but still a good, good friend."

"Is that all you can say?" I stare at the wall, blinking back tears, and then something occurs to me. "But this murder means that the queen won't come — doesn't it?"

"It's too late, poppet," says Valentina, a flickering smile on her face. "She's already here."

Chapter 43

My heart's pounding as I watch Mr Hawkin tell the cast about Ambrose.

"This is a catastrophe. Poor, wonderful Ambrose! We are in mourning — mourning, my sweets."

He stops and looks at the ground. We all look down. I can hear Mrs Hawkin sniffing, and Kwadwo shudders alongside me, containing his tears while mine let rip.

After an indecent pause, Mr Hawkin starts again. "But the show must go on! We have to gather every resource for our royal visitor. We have but days left—"

"You really are the limit, Mr H!" interrupts Bridget. "We lose one of our finest to a murderer and you expect us to rehearse like ... like monkeys for a queen? With her –" she points at Valentina – "as the leading man?"

"Are you scared, Bridget?" asks Valentina. "Scared to perform in front of a queen, or scared you might be next on the murderer's list?"

I look across at Bridget. Her face has gone as pale as her apron.

Chapter 11

That's it. I have to tell someone who can stop the queen visiting the theatre.

I head into the town, using an errand to pick up some posters as an excuse. Back to the spot where Ambrose was found this morning. I hesitate. I don't want to see it. I don't want to see a little puddle of blood that belongs to Ambrose. But it's all cleared up. Washed away. Jameson and Stuart are searching the damp cobbles. When Dog spots them he growls and I have to drag him out of sight.

They're examining the ground as if it might be able to tell them something. Lurking behind a wagon,

I watch them pacing around. What are they looking for?

Jameson is combing every inch, crouching and stepping forward one tiny step at a time. Stuart is picking at the spaces between the cobbles with a stick, flicking out horse droppings and crud. So intense is the search they don't speak to each other at all and they don't notice me.

I squeeze the cloth in my pocket, a shred of red wool. My only evidence. I know they're never going to believe a word I say. But even so, I must try.

I step forwards.

"Here?" says the short one.

"What's that then?" says the other, peering down at the short one's hands.

"Excuse me!" I say, marching up to them. "Excuse me, but—"

"Oooh," says the young one. "That looks like a pin."

"Very nasty," says the short one, holding up one of Valentina's hatpins.

Jameson looks up at me. "What do you want, tiddler?"

"That's—"

Hearing a familiar laugh, I turn.

Valentina's there, right behind me.

"Hello, Mouse," she says. "Out for a little sightseeing?"

I run.

Chapter 15

I don't think I've ever run back to the theatre so fast or been so glad to see Mr Hawkin.

He's talking to a man I've never seen before. He must be very important because Mr Hawkin spends the whole conversation bent double in a courtly bow. I look around for Kwadwo but he's nowhere. I'm going to have to talk to him, and this would be a good moment. But the only person I can find is Adam, who's spying from behind a curtain.

"Who is it?"

"He was Kwadwo's master, apparently," Adam whispers. "He works for the queen. Lord something or other."

"Oh!"

We lie flat on the stage, shoulder to shoulder, watching.

I look at the man. Stuffy, wigged, dry. There's no way he'd believe anything coming out of me.

"Of course, sir, of course," says Mr Hawkin, practically scraping the floor with his nose. "We will scrub every inch, every splinter, every knot and joint of this stage."

"And," says the man, "we will have to have a dressing room for Her Majesty."

"But what about rehearsal?" Mr Hawkin straightens up from his hairpin stance and chances an eyeball-to-eyeball stare with the visitor. "We have a reputation. We cannot simply act our way around a – a—"

"Queen?" interrupts the man.

"Well, yes, despite being a queen – and no doubt a breath from godliness – she may still fluff a line or misplace a fellow thespian. In short, sir, she may throw the performance into chaos…" Mr Hawkin's speech fades away. He stares at the ground, clears his throat, begins a sentence and then fades out before trying again. "We will, of course, work with it. However we may assist."

"And the script by tomorrow afternoon."

With that the visitor rams through the main door of the theatre, letting it swing shut in the wind.

Chapter 16

I take Adam to find Kwadwo, who has closed the door to his quarters and is lurking in the furthest corner, hiding behind a wooden crate.

"Has he gone?" he says, peeking over the box.

"Well gone," I reply. "You're safe."

"Thank the lord," he says, uncurling from his hiding place. "When I saw him I didn't know what to do."

"He'll come back," I say. "Kwadwo, Adam … the murderer is here in the theatre." Now I've said it.

"But the murders didn't happen here," says Adam.

"But they're all connected to here."

"Who?" says Kwadwo. "Who would kill Ambrose?"

I look at them both. I look into my heart and I know that I can trust them.

"Valentina," I mutter.

"No!" says Adam. "It can't be. You've got it all wrong."

But Kwadwo doesn't say anything.

"I have no proof. Nothing but the way she's behaved – and the scrap of wool that you found, Kwadwo. Oh, and some paper, with mud on it." I look from one to the other. They're both open-mouthed.

As I try to explain myself, it all rushes to my mind at once. "It means she's killed three people. Mr Dale, Lady Grey and poor Ambrose."

"But why?" says Adam, his face pulling into the moment before tears. "Why would she need to kill anyone?"

"She's trying to get to the queen."

Adam screws up his face.

"She's trying to kill the queen. She's a…" I struggle for the word. "An assassin."

Adam sits back and stares at me.

"You mean she wants to kill our queen because someone's paid her to do it?"

I nod.

"Who?"

"I don't know – another king or queen or duke.

From somewhere else. Does it matter?"

Adam sniffs. "What about Ambrose? Why did she kill him?"

"Because, like me, he'd guessed that she was the murderer," I say.

"Which puts you in a dangerous situation, Mouse," says Kwadwo under his breath. "Especially if she knows you know."

Footsteps slap on the paving outside and the door swings open. Valentina rushes in, breathless, laughing.

"There you are, little Mouseling – been looking for you everywhere. I want to show you the play I've written."

Chapter 17

It seems that in Valentina's new play, written for the queen, we will be using smoke effects and the ancient trapdoor in the stage.

My heart is now so full of dread I feel like I'm walking in a dream.

"The trapdoor is for Valentina." Mr Hawkin gazes at the rusty hinges, as if imagining Valentina slipping through into the dark recess below. "Now, Mouse, we must work on Her Majesty's costume. And get the smoke chest, child."

Kwadwo looks up from beside the stage. He glances over to Valentina. It's his way of telling me he'll watch her while I'm gone. But is that enough? "Come on, Mouse, upstairs," says Mr Hawkin. "Mrs Hawkin, my dove, if you would assist."

I don't want to leave Valentina. But this is a wonderful opportunity to talk to both the Hawkins away from her. "Coming, Mr H."

I follow him up to the costume store and before he gets a chance to touch a single garment, I corner him. "Mr H – I think there's going to be an attempt on the queen's life while she's here."

Mrs Hawkin half gasps. Mr Hawkin raises an eyebrow. "Where, Mouse, would you get that kind of idea?"

"I think Lady Grey was murdered by Valentina."

"Enough!" he says, holding up his hand. "Valentina is a duchess – she is practically royal herself."

"Exactly. She's connected to people from all over the world. She's got no loyalty to our queen. But every sort of loyalty to another."

"She has a point!" pipes up Mrs Hawkin.

But Mr Hawkin isn't having any of it. "Quiet now, both of you. And no more of this foolishness, Mouse, or you'll be out on your ear." He waves a finger at me. "Understand?"

Furious, I line up all the grandest dresses before he flings his way through them, chucking them into a monstrous pile. Mrs Hawkin picks them up from the floor, shaking her head all the while, a big frown on her face.

"Too big, too small, too badly made. How about this?" He holds up a red velvet dress, stained under the armpits and smelling rough, but looking better than most of the others.

"Will it fit the queen?" I say, too cross to really help him. "Is she tall or short?"

Mr Hawkin's smile fades. "I have no idea. Oh, lord – she might be three foot nothing – or six foot eight. Valentina, Valentina…" He runs out, clutching the dress.

"Mouse," says Mrs Hawkin, holding my elbow for a moment. "Be careful. Valentina is a dangerous creature."

She throws the last rejected gown into a hamper and we both pile down the stairs together lugging the smoke box between us.

At the very bottom, while we're still in the wings, she holds me close and kisses my cheek. "Please, Mouse. Beware of the cat. Let the soldiers do it. Let the soldiers guard the queen."

She lets me go and runs back to her sewing.

Chapter 18

I'm about to check the contents of the smoke chest when I'm spotted by Valentina. It's as if she's got eyes in the back of her head.

"Put it there, Mouse." She points at the back of the stage behind the trapdoor. "Swords!" she shouts.

"Swords!" echoes Mr Hawkin. "Swords!"

Adam looks around with his paintbrush in his hand. "Eve?" he calls. "You're supposed to be doing props!"

Eve thumps over. The graceless fairy. She flings two foils across the stage, one of which hits her mother's foot.

"Eve!" yelps Mrs Hawkin.

Eve stomps away, casting a sad look at Valentina, who doesn't even notice and instead rushes over to me, to poke me with a foil.

"Up, Mouse. You need to fight Mr H on stage, to work out our choreography around where the queen will sit. You are a prince and he is an evil old baron who wants to marry her. Before that, let's see how good you are."

The moment I pick up my blade, she lunges at me. And somehow this feels in earnest. I leap back and she attacks, driving me to the edge of the stage.

"No!" I push forward, catching the point of the steel in her trouser leg.

Valentina jabs, avoiding my blade, nicking my shirt, cutting a small hole in my sleeve. "How's this? Or this?" The rapier swoops past my ear and the corner of my shirt collar flies in the air. "And how about this?" The point of her sword darts into the boards around my feet, forcing me to spring backwards.

She's won, and I feel a surge of anger. Not at her. At myself. I should have seen it coming.

"Valentina, Valentina, have a heart!" says Mr Hawkin, and she lets her steel drop. Her face is all apology.

"I'm sorry – I got carried away. Are you OK, Mouse? Did I hurt you?" With barely a breath she steps forward and hugs me, pinning both my arms so that I can't even lift my blade.

"Valentina!" I say, wriggling to escape.

Letting go, she pokes her delicate little forefinger though the hole in my shirt. "Oops!" she giggles. "More sewing, I suppose." Stepping back, she picks up her rapier. "You've learned a great deal, little one. You are so much better than you were a month ago. Now your turn, Mr H."

"What? Fight Mouse?" Mr Hawkin, who has been reading his lines in the script, looks up. He's evidently appalled.

"Yes," says Valentina. "You may be surprised by her skill."

Valentina gazes at me and I meet her eyes.

She doesn't even smile.

Chapter 49

Afterwards, I feel so filled with dread I sit back on my heels in the shadow and bite back a sudden urge to cry. This is too big. I don't know what to do. Valentina can outwit me at every move. I can't even win a sword fight.

Dog sits on my feet.

An arm lands gently on my shoulder. It's Kwadwo.

A moment later, Adam is at my other side. He sits right up close so that I can smell his biscuity skin smell. The same comforting smell he had when we were little.

I whisper to them about telling Mrs Hawkin and

how unsurprised she was but how useless, and how Mr Hawkin refused to listen. Kwadwo stares over at Valentina.

He pinches his nose between his forefingers, holding his hand there. "She's ruthless."

"All we can do is watch every step she makes," I say.

Adam nods. "And, may I add, there are three of us." He puffs out his chest and smiles his little wonky smile. "Three of us and only one murderer. You're not on your own, Mouse."

Then he leaps to his feet and waves an imaginary sword. "We can watch every step. And we can thwart her!"

Chapter 50

The queen is not going to rehearse with us.

I'm relieved.

The man who once called himself Kwadwo's master comes to the theatre again and, ignoring Mr Hawkin's begging, says, "The script will be with Her Majesty for a day and then the performance will take place. Her Majesty will learn her lines. She will arrive for the play, receive the adulation of a selected audience and leave under cover of darkness."

"There's the small matter of her costume?" asks Mr Hawkin, flapping the sweat-stained dress before the man.

In response the man shakes his head. "Her Majesty will bring her own costume."

Mr Hawkin looks devastated, but I'm not at all surprised.

Until we have the queen, Kwadwo is playing her part. It's the first time I've seen him act. He's good. Very good.

We rehearse from morning till night from then on. I watch Valentina every second, but she never leaves the theatre or does anything suspicious. Adam and Kwadwo watch her too. I go to bed exhausted every night, and every morning Valentina greets me all smiles and all attention.

On the day before the performance, the queen's lord comes back to the theatre to inspect our progress.

"I can't act in front of him – he'll recognise me," says Kwadwo.

Mr Hawkin stares at him. "Very well. Eve shall read the lines. Valentina – act to the chair."

The play is a love story and is a mishmash of all the plays we've ever done. Valentina plays a young man with no money. The queen will play a maiden of means. Her mother, played by Bridget, will want her to marry Mr Hawkin, who is evil and rich. The nasty mother loves her daughter so much, she keeps her in a tower so that she cannot be taken, but plucky

Valentina and her trusty servant – that's me – take the maiden from under her mother's nose, and Valentina and the queen get married in secret. That's what's supposed to happen.

The rehearsal is a shambles. No one comes on or off at the right time. Valentina's trapdoor jams, but Kwadwo cannot be persuaded to fix it under the eye of his one-time master so Valentina has to sneak off the back of the stage using the smoke chest to hide behind. Mr Hawkin insists on putting a mouldy Turkish rug under the queen's chair and then overacts to it. Bridget forgets her lines and Eve looks bored. The scenery shakes. There is a brief cloudburst and the sawdust floor turns to wooden soup.

Incredibly, our visitor lasts until the end and then has a long, whispered conversation with Mr Hawkin.

"She won't come, will she?" I say to Adam. "Surely it's too dangerous. And we're too terrible." The two of us are standing in the wings watching the conversation.

I catch the words *headstrong … foolish … unwise*. The man shakes his head, and incredibly, at the end of their talk, Mr Hawkin swings around to the rest of us and gives us a broad smile. "Yes!" is all he says.

Chapter 51

I barely sleep, but in the early morning I'm wrenched from a dream where I'm drowning by someone banging on the main doors. Opening them a chink, I see Jameson and Stuart standing there. New coats, or clean ones, and boots shiny black.

"Open up!" barks the older one.

I step back, letting them push through.

He stops. "We meet again."

I bare my teeth in a half-grin and, looking over my shoulder to check that Valentina isn't standing there, I say, "I'm very worried for the queen's safety. I think someone might be plotting to kill her."

"So do we," says Jameson. "That's why we're here. Don't worry yourself, tiddler, we'll be checking everything."

"No stone unturned," says Stuart, picking up my plait and making a show of checking underneath.

Thank goodness.

I stand back to let them pass and they march over to the stage, inspecting every part.

I run up to the Hawkins' quarters and bang on their door. Adam answers and I point to the men.

"They're checking everything!"

"I'll get Pa," he says.

They do search everything. Every*one*. I think about the two little bottles somewhere in Valentina's quarters, full of sugar water, and wonder if she'd be able to explain them away. I think about looking for them myself and leaving them on her coverlet again, but there's no time and unfortunately nobody finds them.

"Would you give us a moment's privacy?" announces Valentina. The two men ignore her and sit down to watch our rehearsals. It rattles Valentina. They pick their noses and shuffle and stare and I don't like them either, but I'm so relieved that they're here.

We reach the end and try to be normal. Valentina spends a long time under the stage fiddling with the trapdoor. But Kwadwo checks it afterwards and says there's nothing wrong. More strangers come in, presumably the queen's men, checking seats and examining the structure of the building. They sniff and scrape their fingers along the wood and check for splinters.

"When's the queen going to arrive?" Adam asks. "We start the play soon. How will she know where to be?"

He's right about the play. It's going to be hard to perform with a person who hasn't a clue where to stand or sit, although, to be fair, Valentina has written it so that the queen will spend most of her time sitting on a chair in the middle of the stage. She doesn't even have that many lines.

The door swings open again and my heart jumps, but it's three soldiers in fancy uniforms with wigs and gold braid.

The sky's darkening now, and the seagulls are flying back into land. Distantly, a bell tolls the half hour. We start at nine. Half an hour to go.

Outside the doors, the queen's personally selected audience is getting noisy.

"Do we let them in? Oh, lord!" Mr Hawkin wrings his hands. "This is so awkward. Never in my years have I known a thing be so awkward."

Mr Hawkin's eyes are round and frightened. Even Valentina looks alarmed. Adam has frozen at the back of the stage, and Bridget is reading her lines through as if her life depends on it. Kwadwo has disappeared altogether.

"Supposing she doesn't turn up," says Mr Hawkin, and the feeling of dread that's been building for days practically stops me breathing. Valentina is safely with Mr Hawkin, so I wander up the stairs to examine my make-up and find Valentina's bird bashing itself against the bars.

I reach over, grab the little cage with the tiny bird, take it up to the window above Valentina's bed and open the cage door.

"This is for Ambrose," I say. "And Mr Dale."

The bird hesitates.

"And the woman at the harbour."

"Go on," I say.

It pokes its bill through the doorway, sniffs the air and then hops on to the window ledge. It turns to look at me.

"Fly," I urge.

Spreading its wings, it shudders and pecks once at its breast. I extend my finger to stroke it, but the moment I do, it leaps into the darkness and vanishes.

Chapter 52

The queen is small. Much smaller than I expected, and much smilier than I expected. In fact, she seems quite ordinary.

"Sorry I'm late," she says. "Carriage got stuck in a rut – and then we got lost finding this place. Is my dress all right?"

She holds her arms out in a most unqueenly way, yanking the skirt up so that we can see her legs.

"Oh, Your Majesty," grovels Mr Hawkin. "So fine, so perfect, so incomparably superb. Your taste is impeccable."

The queen glares at him. "So it's all right then? Jolly

good. One of my maids chose it. Hoped she'd got it right. Where do you want me?"

Valentina, who has been motionless for over a minute, springs into life. "This way, Your Majesty. This way to the stage."

"I've learned my lines; pretty sure I've got them down. You must be my lover," the queen giggles. "Daniel? Is that the name?"

"Yes, Your Majesty," says Valentina, standing back and letting the queen mount the stage. "Now, after you've entered, most of your part should centre on or around the chair – but towards the end of the play we will have you seated, if that's agreeable?"

"Yes, all as agreed. I must say this is jolly exciting." The queen claps her hands and tries the chair out. Mr Hawkin brushes me off the stage and shoves me to the side. "Mouse, out of the way – you must get everything ready. Please don't get in the way of our important guest." He shunts me towards my table of props, which I check, and check again. Nothing seems to be amiss. No nasty surprises from Valentina.

Except she is going to try and kill the queen.

The poison isn't poison any more. But there are other ways.

I realise I've been standing and staring for five minutes and the queen is now staring back. "Are you quite well?" she asks, her face a picture of concern.

"I— Yes..." I stammer, and stick my face through the gap in the curtain so that I can see the audience.

"Can I open the doors?" shouts Mrs Hawkin from the floor.

"Of course, of course!" calls Mr Hawkin, and the soldiers and Jameson and Stuart stand, waiting for the audience.

There's a rumble as the doors are opened but then, as they enter, the crowd goes oddly quiet, whispering to each other rather than the usual shouting.

"Where is she?"

"What does she look like?"

"How will we know which one she is?"

The curtains are still drawn so they can't see anything different, except for soldiers where there would normally be stallholders.

I expected a collection of the gentry. Instead the queen seems to have invited every low life in Bristow. I even see the three boys who chased me into the harbour. The soldiers look shocked. These are the people who can't normally come to the theatre. They're even less lovely than our usual scabby crowd.

They dribble through, and each one is searched for knives or pistols. No bottles or eggs allowed. I see a bag of shopping taken from a woman, and a sack of something wriggling. Crabs? Audiences have strange ways of showing their disgust, but they remain very quiet. It's eerie.

"Where's Eve?" I ask Adam. "She didn't get me to help with her wings."

"Up there." He points to the heavenly balcony where Eve's sitting on the side waiting to swing over the stage. She almost smiles. I almost smile back.

The queen stands behind the curtain. Valentina is talking to her but I have to warn Her Majesty.

I swallow down my nerves and sidle along towards the queen.

"Mouse, what are you doing here?" Valentina gives me a shove back into the wings. I push back but Valentina's too strong and my feet slide on the boards.

"Your Majesty," I begin.

"Shut up, duckling!" hisses Valentina. I see the flash of a knife in her hand and feel the steel on my cheek.

I step back. So she plans to stab the queen.

Adam shuffles alongside me as we wait for our cue. I point at Valentina and mime a knife. He nods, his eyes wide. We're supposed to be two boys who fool around at the front of the stage throwing acrobatics while Kwadwo changes the scenery behind us. I'm going to have to think of a way of using our antics to get the knife from Valentina.

"You're on!" hisses Mr Hawkin, and Adam and I tumble on to the stage, falling over each other, rolling and leaping and getting a round of applause from the audience. I avoid his heel and he misses my elbow. Valentina appears on the stage behind us and we swing around so that Adam's feet flail in the air, whacking Valentina on the chin. She stumbles and I take the second that she's down to whisk the knife from her belt. We bound off as Mr Hawkin sweeps on, hiding behind his villainous cloak.

As she recovers from her fall, Valentina shoots me a look of such raw hatred that my knees give way beneath me.

I stagger to the side and I've barely caught my breath before Bridget's hissing at me and I realise I'm on for the sword fight. Adam takes the knife, and I swap my short jacket for a long one and swish my blade through the air. It whips and flexes and I feel sicker than I've ever felt before.

"Go!" Adam pushes me on stage and I leap into my starting position, holding my sword in front of me. Mr Hawkin appears from the other side of the stage, and I skirt the trapdoor in the floor to meet him. He flashes the briefest of smiles before bellowing at me, "What pipsqueak is this? What tiny vermin? What gossamer?" He swipes the air and I leap back, shouting something vaguely similar to my lines.

At the back of the stage, the queen emerges from the curtain and sits on the chair. The audience cheer and whoop, and the queen waves. As we fight around her, she does a fair job of looking scared, leaping backwards as we spring forwards and putting her hands up in fear. The audience roar as we clash swords over her head and I hear shuffling as the soldiers move closer, but we move on, dancing back and forth, clashing, flicking, circling.

I become aware of someone moving close to the queen. It's Valentina. They're supposed to run away together; I'm supposed to be holding Mr Hawkin back. He drives me closer to the front of the stage, blades clash and the audience *oooh* and *ahh!*

We circle, our swords locked, the hilts touching, our noses almost touching. It's about time for the smoke to begin and, bang on cue, behind the queen's chair, Valentina leans in through the trapdoor. I hear the strike of the tinderbox.

"Aaah!" shouts Mr Hawkin, pushing my blade down so that I nearly lose it, but I hang on and drive him back another pace.

"Yay!" shouts the crowd.

"Do for 'im, little 'un!" shouts a woman. "Go ooon!"

As I batter Mr Hawkin back across the stage I notice a smell of burning. It doesn't smell like the salts we use for the smoke effects; it smells of pitch and pine cones. I need to stop and look, but Mr Hawkin keeps fighting, so I have to fight back, pushing him harder and harder, our eyes and swords locking and breaking and slipping.

"Mr H," I hiss. "Something's wrong." But he's really getting into this and suddenly I'm fighting for my life. Around us the smoke's getting thicker. I glance down. It's billowing up from the trapdoor. I look towards the queen. She's still sitting but she's coughing madly and waving the smoke away from her face. The soldiers aren't doing anything because they know about the smoke. But they don't know that this is the wrong smoke.

Clever Valentina.

"Mr H! Stop a minute!" I yelp, but he keeps going.

I parry and thrust, buying myself a second to sneak another look at the queen. Valentina is crouching alongside, giving her some water.

Water? I lose a second staring at Valentina's hand. She's got a tiny blue bottle in it. The one that should contain poison, but actually contains sugar water. I hope.

Mr Hawkin jabs me in the ribs. "Avast!" he shouts.

I turn. "Mr H! Stop! Just stop!" I shout, and flick his sword out of his hand and into the audience. He stands open-mouthed, staring into his empty hand.

The audience roars. I race across the stage towards Valentina.

She looks up. A sweet little smile crosses her mouth. Blowing me a kiss she whispers, "Sorry, Mouse. You were good, but not good enough." The little blue bottle bounces off my thigh as she leaps through the trapdoor to vanish underneath the smouldering stage.

Chapter 53

It takes a moment for the smoke chest to light and for coloured flames to burst across the whole stage, and a second longer for the audience to realise they're not for show and to panic. Shrill screams race through the crowd as fast as the tiny flames leap across the boards.

"What the—" Mr Hawkin steps forwards, but a wall of flame shoots from the wooden planks surrounding the trapdoor. Screams ring out through the theatre and the main doors crash open. Smoke billows from the stage, thick and grey and impossible to see through. Sparks shoot into the air. I try to step closer to the queen, who is coughing and spluttering.

I could maybe just about reach her but it's already getting scarily hot. Mr Hawkin tries to approach from the other side, but he's forced back by the heat. Beyond the smoke, she clambers on to her chair while the flames advance.

"We'll have to go from the back!" I shout over the screams of the audience.

And then the sky falls. Kwadwo's scenery drops, plunging into the flames that surround the queen. Orange stars of new fire blossom across the canvas.

"No!" I shout.

"By Jupiter!" I hear Mr Hawkin and I look up. There, suspended above the flames is Eve. She's wearing her wings, her face reflecting the flames, a look of horror on her face.

"No!"

"Save me – Mama, Papa! Save me!"

The queen looks up. "Who's that?" she shouts, trying to stand.

"She's mad!" shouts Bridget, leaping past me and throwing herself into the audience. Mr Hawkin has vanished. I'm the only person left on the stage. The queen has got caught up in the legs of her chair; she's struggling to get out. Above me, Eve swings, twenty feet above certain death. I glance into the audience. The soldiers have run. I can't see Jameson and Stuart and the flames are getting bigger, hotter.

Smokier.

"Mouse!" yells Eve. I look up as the smoke billows around her. "Help me!"

I don't reply. There's no point. What do I do? I can't save everyone. I can only save one.

Chapter 54

"Mouse!" I hear someone behind me. It's Adam. He's holding a bucket of water that's almost as big as he is. "Mind out!" he yells, and he chucks it over the flames. For a second the fire retreats, turning instead into a cloud of steam that swamps the stage and balloons up to hide Eve and the queen.

"I'll get Eve," he calls through the babble. "You save the queen!"

"Adam – be careful!" I shout.

"You be careful, Mouse!" he replies, and he races off up the stairs at the side of the theatre.

A second later his mother rushes in, also with a

bucket of water and flings it at the stage, but it's not enough. She stops for a second, looking up at her daughter, and then runs for the same set of stairs as Adam.

Patches of canvas are burning, tiny flames eating their way through towards the queen and then puffing out as they reach her. What? Her island of the stage is not actually on fire – I don't understand until I remember the disgusting rug that Mr Hawkin insisted on laying down under her chair. It's damp, like everything, and it won't burn, just smoulder. I look up above my head. Eve's still there, swinging like a pendulum through the smoke. She's coughing and crying and the flames are licking at her wings. A flaming angel.

"Eve," I shout, hurdling a line of flames that are establishing themselves across the middle of the stage. "Undo your rope! Jump!"

In spite of the roar of the fire and the screaming of the audience, I can hear her. Her angel voice, clear as a bell: "I'm going to die!"

"Well, die then!" I shout up, as I reach the stinky old rug that's under the queen's chair.

"Mouse," says Eve, her voice still clearer than the air we're breathing.

"No. I'm sorry, Eve – I'm too busy!" I shout as I reach the queen. "Your Majesty!" My words are eaten by the crackling flames. "Your Majesty!"

At first she doesn't move and I wonder if Valentina has successfully poisoned her. That somehow I didn't manage to wash out the bottle. That she bought a third bottle of poison. But then she coughs, spits and opens one eye. She raises a hand, but it's feeble. She's struggling to breathe. Reaching through the smoke to the royal armpits I try to drag her. She's small but she's very heavy and all I succeed in doing is flipping her on to the carpet. Tiny flames break out around the rug and I stamp on them but as fast as I stamp, the flames spring up somewhere else.

It's so hot.

Reaching under her armpits again I pull and pull. The rug comes too.

The smoke is getting thicker and I can only dimly see my hands. I can only just breathe.

Come on, Mouse.

I can't possibly do this.

Yes, I can.

Hooking my arms right under the queen's armpits and clasping my hands across her chest I pull her upright, or almost upright, and walk backwards. Behind the smoke is a wall of raging orange. The whole of the backstage must now be alight.

One step.

Two steps.

A length of flaming canvas collapses across the stage to my right.

One step.

Two steps.

I'm halfway across. The noise is extraordinary.

One step.

Two steps.

Suddenly a pair of strong hands join mine.

Kwadwo.

"I'll take her head. Grab her feet!" he yells.

The flames are so high they leap over her boots. Working together, we lug her right across the stage where the imaginary fires of Hell have become pillars of sparks shooting up from below. I glance over my shoulder. The theatre is a ring of fire and we're right in the middle.

At the edge of the stage, he jumps down and rolls her into his arms.

Through the steam, Kwadwo points towards the heavens above the stage. "I've got her. Run." I follow the direction of his gaze. High up in the eaves, surrounded by smoke and flames, stands Valentina. I can't see her face; everything is orange. Everything's on fire.

Boom.

Chapter 55

I'm blown sideways. Deafened.

I can't work out which way is up, and smoke and cinders fill my head.

For a second the fire pauses, and then resumes with more passion and anger than before, and all that's left of the queen's chair is splinters and a huge hole. I glance over my shoulder. Kwadwo is carrying the queen over the sawdust floor, his bare feet stamping on the tiny strings of flames racing from stage to wall and back to stage. He's nearly at the side of the theatre, heading for a new hole where the wall used to be.

Looking up, the thatched roof is well alight. Only a small patch directly above the stage is untouched. And there's no sign of Valentina. Or Adam. Or Eve.

"Adam!" I shout, although my voice is whisked away by the searing heat.

Eve's rope has burned away.

"Adam!"

Frantically I comb the burning structure for any sign of life and then I see him, little Adam, Eve slung between him and his mother, both struggling down a long ladder at the side of the theatre. As he nears the bottom, he shouts.

"Go after Valentina. Get her. And take this." He throws the short dagger I took from Valentina earlier. "It's what I used to cut Eve down. But it's sharp."

I hesitate for a second, staring down at the shiny blade.

He actually thinks I could use it.

"Stick it in your belt. Now, go, Mouse – go."

I race round the stage and glance back across the theatre before plunging into the smoke. The last I see is Adam, Mrs Hawkin and Kwadwo pouring water over the queen and Eve, Dog licking the queen's face and all of them surrounded by flames.

Chapter 56

There's only one way Valentina could have got out of the theatre, and that's through a tiny door at the very back which leads up a metal staircase to the top of the gallery and out on to a platform that overlooks the river. As I race up the smoke-filled twisted passage, I wonder if I'm mad. When the fire takes hold on this side, I will have to jump. There's no other way. But as I emerge on to the platform I can guess exactly where she is. There's a ship. *The Running Stag*. It's moving at a snail's pace down the river, poled along by the sailors, the sails floppy on the spars. She must have jumped on to one of the masts. It would be around the right height. I look at the distance. Could I jump that?

It's too far.

I can't make it, but I can make the river.

Not letting myself think, I jump into the filthy water below. My nose fills and I fizz down under the surface before fighting my way back up, coughing and spluttering, but the water's not cold and I strike out for the ship. No one will have seen me. It's an easy few strokes downstream to the back of the boat. I stop there for a second, holding on to a huge net that seems to be slung across the back of the ship.

It's easy to grapple my way up and a minute later I'm clinging, dripping, to the top of the stern. There's nobody on this part of the deck so I swing my leg over the top and crouch, searching for a sign of Valentina.

Where would she be? I don't know my way around a ship at all so, holding Adam's dagger in one hand, I open doors. A horseshoe of small cabins opens on to the deck. Some with dull amber light; most of them utterly dark. Each time I try a door, my heart jams slightly further up my throat until inside the last room I find a sword stand. Closing the door behind me, I fumble in the dark, trying out the swords. They're heavy. Much heavier than my little foil, but they're also much longer. Weighing them and trying a lunge, I choose the lightest, which is still much heavier than I'm used to.

Dagger in my pocket, sword in my hand, I creep out and crouch by the balustrade on the side of the ship, away from the flames. Although most of the crew are leaning over the side, silhouetted against the orange flames, poling the ship along, another small group cluster around the wheel. Among them is a tall broad man, Captain Teach, and a tall slender man. Valentina.

I breathe in and out, trying to steady the rhythm, then I step forward.

"Valentina!" I shout.

"Mouse?" She turns, and in the light of the fire I can see the gleam of her eyes. "Oh, lambkin. I'm so glad you're not burning up in there but why are you here?"

I swallow. "To stop you. You're a murderer."

"Oh, sweetie, that's a horrid word. I'm an assassin." She steps towards me and I see the gleam of something passed to her by the captain.

"You killed Lady Grey."

"I did, clever Mouse."

"And you let Walter take the blame."

"Poor Walter."

"And Mr Dale?"

"Oh, dear. Yes, that was unfortunate. But that wasn't actually me. I just—"

"And Ambrose."

"Oh, that one hurt, sweetie. I adored Ambrose – but he was too close for comfort."

"So you killed them."

"It's what I do." She giggles. "Didn't you know? Hadn't you worked it out?"

"I thought you were an actress!" I shout, bringing my blade around so that she can see it.

"I am, of sorts. Making strangers fall in love with me, dancing and fighting on cue – sometimes on the stage, sometimes not." She unsheathes a sword that looks bigger and shinier than the one I'm holding.

"Are you sure you're ready for this, duckling?"

"Fight! Fight! Fight!" chime the sailors.

"Get this over with, Valentina," says the captain.

"You really should run..."

"No – I won't."

"Are you sure? Aren't you out of your depth?"

I shake my head.

"Well, if you think so. Come on then, Mouse. What have you learned? Enough to beat me? Hmm?"

This is mad. I'm mad.

"What you did was wrong, Valentina. Evil."

"Of course it was wrong – I never pretended it

wasn't." She climbs up a set of steps that take her closer to the main mast. "But you always knew I did wrong things. Didn't you? You always knew I wasn't perfect."

Is this a trap? It may be, but I follow, and the sailors part to let me through.

"She a child?" says one to another.

"Reckon," comes the reply.

"We should stop this," says a third. "She's only a tiddler."

"Get out of my way," I snarl, and the sailors step back as I leap on to the deck. I'm pleased to see Valentina step back as if I've startled her.

"*En garde*, little rabbit," she says.

I don't say anything. I drop to a crouch, letting the sword feel heavy and close in my hand. It's too dark to watch her elbow twitch, I'll have to rely on my instincts. But then, she'll have to rely on hers.

"The queen's not in there, you know," I say.

"What do you mean?" she answers, her eyes on mine.

"We got her out. Kwadwo got her out. He carried her through the flames. Oh, and the poison in the bottle – I replaced it with sugar water. She only passed out because of the smoke."

I hear a tiny gasp of irritation and I know I've got

to her and I lunge.

She parries.

I advance again and she flicks my blade to the side. It's heavy and I find it hard to hold it out for longer than a second. I'm going to lose it if I can't keep it close to my body.

We circle and she attacks. Fast, furious and deadly. I feel the edge of her blade cut into my jacket. Did it reach my skin? I don't know. I've heard that if the blade is really sharp you don't feel it. I slip back behind the mast and swing from side to side.

"What are you up to, Mouse? What's your plan? You can't think you'll kill me, kitten – I'm your teacher."

I don't know what I'm up to but everything is fizzing. My anger is driving my limbs in a way I didn't know they could move. Without a thought I grab the spar above me with one hand and flip myself up so that I'm standing on a thin, round beam, looking down at Valentina's head.

Her eyes widen as I lunge, and she staggers backward. I attack again. She grabs a rigging ladder and two paces later she's up with me, both of us standing on the thin spar.

The sailors roar, but I don't take my eyes off her. There's no circling up here; we have only back and forth, up and down. There's another spar above me and I could leap for it, I could go on leaping up the ship if I have to, but what will happen when we reach the top?

Chapter 57

I don't have to make the decision. Valentina goes first. She grabs a rope and hauls herself up the rigging again until she's balanced above me. Her blade swings past my ear, chopping a chunk from my hair.

"No!" I shout, tucking my sword across my stomach and flipping the length of the wooden beam. At the end is a loose rope and I grip it under my knee to push out from the spar, bouncing against the sail on the next mast along. If I can get there I'll be able to race her up to the crow's nest at the top. The rope I'm on stretches and I spring back to the first mast. Valentina swipes at me, cutting a hole in my jacket.

"Whoa!" shout the sailors below.

I push again and this time make it to the next mast. "Jump, child!" someone yells, and I throw myself off the rope to the sail attached to the spar. Slipping, falling, thumping, the furled sail catches me and, sword in hand, I sit up at the same time as Valentina jumps across from her mast to mine.

The sailors cheer and whoop and I raise the sword as she's flying through the air and knock her off the beam.

"Mouse!" she shouts. "That's unfair." But I can tell from her voice she's enjoying this.

"You betrayed me!" I yell, balancing on the spar and bent at the knee, waiting for her to land.

"I didn't!" she exclaims. "I tried to keep you out of it." She lands and her blade slices down towards my foot. I leap backwards, my feet steady on the wood.

"You sent me to buy poison – you told them I was coming."

"That aside, I really did try to keep you safe."

"I trusted you!" I shout.

"I'm sorry. You shouldn't have found out; you shouldn't have cared." Valentina hooks one arm around a rope and uses it to swing out towards me, swiping, cutting, slicing.

There's a sudden flash and a crack overhead, and the soft sound of rain dims the roar of the theatre fire. For a second, Valentina looks up, and I use that second to jump past her blade to the rigging ladder next to the mast. Before she has a chance to stop me I'm above her again and this time I'm not going to let her past.

"But you looked after me. You told me stories. You fed me. You taught me so much."

She laughs and our swords clash.

"I knew you'd got too close. I tried to drive you away. You should never have put any faith in me, but it was too easy; you were my doll. My poppet. My soft little rabbit." Her sword flashes in the orange light of the flames. "You should have run to Kwadwo when Walter was imprisoned – not me. That was your mistake, not mine!"

"How was I to know you were – so – so..." Anger gives me strength. I push her back, flashing my heavy blade back and forth, faster, harder, it flies through the air.

"Untrustworthy? Oh!" says Valentina as I nearly whisk her sword from her hand. "Clever!" she shouts, leaning forward and driving me back.

"You would have let us burn. Let Walter die." I drive the blade, slicing her shirt, the steel ringing. "What kind of monster are you?"

"Ha!" she shouts, reaching for a rope and swinging out on to the other mast. "Me? What kind of monster? A paid one — just like any soldier. I am a woman in a man's world. But you..." She swings her blade wildly, slashing at the ropes around me. "You will be forever a soft little cub, until you stop caring so much!" Her sword catches mine, whipping it from my hand so that it arcs down out of sight to thump into the deck below.

"No!" I shout.

"See, Mouse?" she says sadly. "You just aren't tough enough."

Her rope swings out, the pendulum even, and I reach for the knife in my belt.

"I am not a soft little cub," I rage. "I am Mouse."

And the world goes into slow motion as I reach my arm as far as it will go, the weight of the tiny blade so unbearably heavy that I think I'll drop it, and I slice. I cut the rope that holds her.

Her hands close on the rope and her sword tumbles, hitting the deck below us.

Valentina looks up, her mouth in an O, her eyebrows surprised.

Her fall is lit by the flames from the theatre, down, down. It seems to take forever. And I wait for the

thump. But there is no thump.
Only a splash.
And silence.

Chapter 58

A moment later and the sailors swarm.

"Where is she?"

There are so many of them, appearing like ants from the bottom of the ship. With Teach in their midst. I know I must run. And fast.

One side of the mast is still reflecting the orange of the theatre flames, so I make myself beanpole thin on the other side. As the sailors race up, I drop down, one rope then another and within a minute I hit the deck. The ship hasn't moved since I boarded, and with the fear of a thousand angry sailors at my back I race across it and slip head first into the water.

Expecting to find Valentina at any moment, I struggle through the river. Bobbing things bounce against me and under my feet weed drags at my ankles. The theatre wharf is close though, and it takes only a few moments to reach it.

Hauling myself up on to the bank I stop immediately. The searing heat coming off the theatre dries my face instantly. The whole ring of the outside is on fire but the little moth pennant is still flying from the rooftop.

A chain of people with buckets has formed from the river to the building. There's not a chance though. Unless the rain gets really heavy, it's going to burn all the way to the ground. Sparks whoosh into the air, high above the building, and everything roars.

"Kwadwo!"

"Dog!"

"Adam!"

My words vanish into the heat. Silhouettes run between me and the flames. More people with buckets but no one I recognise.

"Kwadwo!" I shout.

My clothes are steaming, it's so hot. But I must find them. Stumbling around the side of the building, I get to the mud patch between the theatre and the warehouses. I stare up at the theatre. Even the pennant is on fire.

"Kwadwo!"

"Adam!"

Behind me, a horse snickers and I turn to see a small group clustered around a carriage with two nervous horses stamping and rearing held by a terrified groom.

Could that be the queen's carriage?

One of the figures is tall and thin. "Kwadwo!"

Avoiding the firefighters I sprint over the mud towards the carriage. As I run, a dark shape breaks from the group and gallops towards me.

"Dog!"

He yaps and leaps and I let my arms fall around his neck and breathe in the smell of burned hair that lies on top of the real smell of Dog.

"Mouse?"

"Adam?"

"Mouse!" He holds me. His tears, his sniffs. Laughter and crying all mixed together. "I thought we'd lost you. I couldn't bear it."

I hold him. We stand so close we make a single fire shadow on the mud.

"Er, excuse me." Someone taps me on the shoulder. It's Jameson, the stubble-haired man. "Her Majesty would like to see you."

"Me?"

"C'mon." Adam hooks his arm in mine and we

walk towards the carriage. I'm vaguely aware that I'm half-wet, half-dry and that I must look like I've been through an underwater bonfire.

"Mouse — is this Mouse?" says the queen. She's sitting in the doorway of the carriage with Kwadwo sitting on the step below her. She's wearing a petticoat and the stubble-man's jacket. She looks as much like the queen as I do.

"My dear, you've been an absolute wonder. A hero. I owe you everything!"

I curtsy. Isn't that what I'm supposed to do?

The queen laughs. "Thank you, child. Thank you for dragging me from the inferno. The smoke quite overcame me and I would have been utterly done for. Now, Kwadwo here tells me that your fellow, Walter, is banged up in Newgate and in need of a pardon."

"Yes," I say, fireworks going off in my head. "He is. He's accused of killing Lady Grey."

"Poor dear Margaret Grey. That was quite dreadful. She was, I think, trying to gather intelligence about an assassin, and a ship. *The Antler, The Stag* or something. The exact thing quite escapes me." The queen sniffs and wipes her nose on Jameson's jacket. "But I gather from him over there —" she points at Stuart — "that your leading lady might be our killer?"

"Er, yes," I say.

"How wonderfully intriguing. What a shame I didn't get to know her better. She sounds terrific."

"She was trying to kill you, Your Majesty," says Kwadwo.

"Yes, but people are always trying to kill me and they're not usually so interesting." She pulls the jacket tighter across her chest. "It's very boring to always be in fear of one's life. Every king in Europe wants my head; they've got assassins in all the ports. So where is she? What's happened to her?"

"I saw her fall off the spar of the ship into the water," I say.

A small sob erupts from my feet, beneath the carriage. I peer down. Huddled by the wheels is a pale figure, hanging on to Kwadwo's leg. It's Eve. All wet and singed. "Is Valentina dead?" she asks.

"I don't know. I'm not sure." And I'm not – I can't believe it. But the queen is relaxing and seems to be enjoying our company, and Jameson and Stuart are here, so I begin to relax too.

She's talking to Kwadwo. "So you're a runaway?"

Kwadwo's nodding. "I was. A long time ago."

"He needs his freedom," says Adam very quickly. And then adds, "Please, Your Majesty."

"Of course," says the queen. "You shall have it. Jameson – my sword, if you please?"

Jameson comes over and passes the queen a small shining sword.

"Kneel, Kwadwo," she says, and then she looks up. "Oh!"

I swing round.

Chapter 59

Valentina. Bloodied and wild and with her hair steaming. But still Valentina.

She's holding a sword in one hand and a lance in the other. One of the theatre lances. Mr Hawkin bought them cheap off a trader a week or so back. They've still got sharp points. Very sharp.

We all back away. Kwadwo stands in front of the queen. I run and stand beside him.

"You'll have to go through us," he says.

Adam joins us. "And me," he says.

I glance over to Jameson. He's fumbling around for a sword, but he doesn't look like he'll be up to

Valentina's standard.

Valentina pulls herself tall.

I reach into my belt for the dagger. But I must have dropped it.

"Mouse!" shouts the queen, and she throws her sword to me.

I catch it, weigh it in my hand and flex it through the air. It's perfect.

I'm exhausted, but something surges through me, giving me strength and focus, and I watch Valentina's blade. Using the lance, she jabs at Kwadwo. He tries to grab the end, but Valentina's fast and she whisks it out of his hand and past him towards the queen. Adam leaps for it, hanging on to the pole until, with a squeal of irritation, Valentina drops it.

"I've got the lance," shouts Adam.

"Hooray for you, little Adam baby," says Valentina, not taking her eyes from mine. "Go on then, Mouse – kill me!" She lowers her sword. "You can't, can you?"

"I'd rather you faced a court," I say, holding the queen's sword steady.

I sense the flick in her elbow first, and lunge before she does, so we clash, sword to sword, hilt to hilt.

She pushes up and away and I manage to hang on to my sword as she barges it to the side.

"No!" I shout, somersaulting over her blade and

stabbing at her from the right.

"Very clever!" she replies, leaping back from me and slicing towards my feet.

I stamp on her blade, and for a second I have the advantage but she pulls and I stumble and we're back circling each other. Behind her, figures move. The queen is now inside the carriage with the door shut, accompanied by Eve. The two soldiers are either side, only one with a sword. The lance is balanced on the window frame, the front end of it in Eve's hands. She's crying – her face is wet but her singed wings and white dress make her look like some kind of magnificent fallen angel. Kwadwo beckons me; he's holding a fishing net. I try to manoeuvre Valentina so that she has her back to the carriage. It's not easy and we clash several times in a moment.

I yell as her blade flicks against my ear.

Warm blood trickles down my face.

"No!" I shout, and I drive, once, twice, three times towards her. She backs up, dancing, laughing.

"Oh, Mouse! You idiot – you'll never beat me!"

Her sword cuts through the air, slicing past my ear and then, quite suddenly dropping.

Time stops.

There's a terrible unearthly cry. It came from Eve.

I look to see what's happened.

It's the lance. Valentina's backed into it.

Eve was holding the shaft.

But the point is sticking out of Valentina's shirt.

"No!" I shout, dropping my sword and running towards her. "No!"

I put my hands on the spreading blood. Faster thicker, warmer than any stage blood.

"Thank you for trying," says Valentina, kneeling. "Sorry, but you're too late, Mouseling."

Her eyes stay open as she falls.

They reflect the fire. Red, like her hair.

Chapter 60

As dawn breaks, the queen thanks us and leaves, promising to meet us later, and then a small hearse arrives.

Two men lift Valentina's body on to a stretcher.

With infinite care, Kwadwo straightens her clothes, folding her arms over the ugly bloodstain.

Her tears mixing with the river water, Eve washes her feet.

They let me arrange her hair.

When I've finished, I look down on to her face. Perfect. Almost smiling.

After she's gone, Adam holds my hand and his

sister's and together we sit watching the embers. The theatre's no more than a skeleton now. The spars reach up to the sky, each one tagged by flames. The whole of the outside has gone and the doorway's a gaping mouth that leads into the centre.

Looking through, I can still see the outline of the stage, but now Hell seems to have overtaken everything.

We don't speak. There's nothing we can say.

That afternoon we sit with the queen in a small annexe of the castle. Her Majesty is issuing orders to astonished officials. The man who once called himself Kwadwo's master is glaring at his one-time servant, who is reading a book and eating grapes. The soldiers have been sent back to Newgate to extract Walter. Mr Hawkin is sitting at the end of the table hugging Eve, who is crying and hugging him back. Mrs Hawkin looks refreshed and puzzled. There is food. So much food, but I find I'm more thirsty than anything else.

Adam talks but I don't think I'm listening. All I can see is Valentina. Her face, her eyes, her smile.

"She could have saved herself," he mutters.

"She could," I say in the end.

"Do you think Eve did it on purpose – you know, the spear?"

I look across at Eve, nestled on her father's lap,

laughing, smiling – actually happy.

"I don't know," I say. "We'll never know, and I don't think even she knows, but I do think, Adam, that you saved her, and you've all proved you love her. Look at her now; she's going to be fine."

Eve sees me looking and sends me a proper, broad, friendly smile, and no matter that at times I could cheerfully have doused her in the river, I smile back, with all my heart.

Epilogue

A week later, possibly the strangest week of my life, and my world has changed.

Valentina is gone. Ambrose is gone. But Walter is back.

Yesterday, on the stormiest day of the early autumn, we buried Valentina next to Ambrose in a corner of St Mary's. The wolfish wind howled over our heads and chewed the leaves from the lime trees, scattering the churchyard with green confetti. We were all there, the Moth troupe, but there were wealthy strangers present who arrived in silent carriages and departed without saying anything. Bridget watched them and sniffed her disapproval. Mrs Hawkin held hands with Eve and Adam. I held hands with Kwadwo and Walter.

There was no sign of Captain Teach. He was probably halfway to the New World.

The priest talked about ashes and dust, and Mr Hawkin whispered alongside him, huge tears running down the valleys on his cheeks. Even Bridget cried.

When the tears stopped, I stepped forwards and dropped a small posy of flowers on each grave. Not ordinary daisies, but Michaelmas daisies, rich purple. The ones that mean farewell. I didn't get them on purpose. They were growing along the riverbank and they looked Valentina-perfect, so I picked them. It was Mrs Hawkin who told me what they meant.

As everyone took their turn flinging earth down on the coffins, I half expected Valentina to appear at the side of the grave. It seemed too big an event for her to miss it, and I imagined her, weeping but exquisite, throwing an orange flower on to my purple daisies. I looked around, but it was Walter at my side, a handkerchief in his hand.

When we turned to get out of the rain, I couldn't believe that the brightness had gone.

And now I sit on Walter's feet, in the middle of the charcoal ring that was the theatre, listening to his stories from inside the prison. Adam and

Eve are alongside their mother and, hooting with uncontrollable giggles, Mrs Hawkin slides off her stool when Walter imitates the gaoler. We all laugh with her. Between us is a campfire of the remaining splinters of the old building made by Bridget and Mr Hawkin, and my feet are warm. It smells of smoked fish and Christmas. And I can't get used to being able to see right through the walls.

Dog lies alongside me, sneezing when the ash blows over us.

Mr Hawkin, Mrs Hawkin, Walter – very thin, but clean-shaven and smiling – Eve, Adam, Bridget and Kwadwo are the new theatre company. The building is to be rebuilt at royal expense, will be called the Phoenix, and we will be the Queen's Players. Walter will play the leading woman, until one day, perhaps, I will grow into it. Kwadwo, now given his liberty, is to be the leading man.

Eve can still play the angel, but this time, more angelic.

Mr Hawkin is delighted. He has bought himself a new coat and Mrs Hawkin a new hat, on credit.

"I think we should write a fresh play," says Mr Hawkin, strutting through the charcoal. "I think we should in some way celebrate the rebirth – the renaissance – of our fair cabinet of imagination.

I think we should recognise the travails, the recent … turbulence, the highs the lows…"

Walter picks up a penny whistle and plays a jaunty tune in time with Mr Hawkin's words.

Mr Hawkin dances a little jig.

He stops and looks across at Adam, who is laughing.

"You look so funny, Father. Just so funny."

"Do I?" says Mr Hawkin.

"You do, Husband," says Mrs Hawkin. "Quite absurd. You are quite the most absurd man."

"And you, quite the most absurd woman," says Mr Hawkin, embracing her.

And they dance, we all dance, arm in arm, heart to heart, as the last orange of the sunset is squashed by a violet cloud.

We dance around the fire. We dance alone; we dance as a family.

Faster and faster we dance our way into a new theatre. New lives.

And here I am, no one's poppet, or duckling, or squirrel, or doll.

No one's little pet.

I, Mouse, have found true love, and having found it I will love those around me and defend them to the end of my days.

Historical Note

It was the late great Joan Aiken who proved that history could be rearranged to accommodate story.

Within this book you will find names and places that do properly belong in the reference section, but they have drifted away from their moorings. There was a pirate, known as Blackbeard, whose real name was Edward Teach and who came from Bristol. But I have put words in his mouth and placed him on a ship and in a time that never existed. There was indeed a Queen Anne I, but never a Queen Anne II.

And Mouse lives in a town almost exactly like Bristol. It has Bristol's strangely named quays, Bristol's pubs and Bristol's infamous Newgate Prison. The real Bristol was a thriving port, sugar did boil out of the doorways, but the Moth Theatre is a thing of dreams. By the imaginary time that this is set, some point in the early eighteenth century, theatres had changed from being open air to indoors. Built of wood, the old ones had either burned down or been repurposed. But what if...?

And so the Moth was born.

Acknowledgements

My name is on the cover, but no book appears fully formed. Instead, the words between the covers have to be calmed, encouraged, coaxed and trimmed, hacked, silenced and transformed. It can be a painful process, but editors are there to wave magic wands at times of crisis and I have been lucky enough to work on this book with two such magicians. Fiona Scoble and Kirsty Stansfield, thank you both, for your conjuring and your clear heads.

Thank you, Kate Shaw, for reading many drafts and for being wise.

And sensitivity reader Alex Sheppard, for pointing things out and for putting me right.

My family too, who discussed through lockdown after lockdown the possibilities of Mouse's path until you were sick to death. Rosa, I'm grateful that we explored Bristol in a way that was not your way. Not a single cafe was open.

And thank you, Ben Mantle, for another gorgeous cover, and all the crew at Nosy Crow for turning the whole story from something insubstantial into something real that belongs in the hands of a child.

I love it, and the nine-year-old me is doing cartwheels across the kitchen.